Promise Of The Wolf

Wolf

Book 2 of The Wolf Pack Series

Alice E Wright

Alice E Wright

Contents

Shake And Rattle And Roll

The whole building shakes as if a beggar shaking a tin can. Back and forth with a bit of rolling just like a carnival ride. I can hear the popping of what I am not sure, but it can't be good. The kids haven't left for school yet. We are running a bit behind schedule today. Josh isn't home from work but he comes in a bit later sometimes. Cop work is like that I've learned. Standing in my bright little kitchen grabbing lunch sacks, it happens. Our amazing historic home was originally built in 1911 and thus missed the "big one" of 1906. We bought this when we were first married as a fixer upper and together, we've turned this ancient relic into a beautiful modern home in the heart of San Francisco. The garage is underneath us, housing our laundry machines and my husband's 4x4. It's an older vehicle, but like this house has been babied and well loved.

The rolling ground causes cracks to appear in the drywall and the kids have come running into the kitchen, wide eyed looking to me for reassurance. This is going on much longer than a normal earthquake. I am getting concerned. I can see a pipe has broken outside and there is a visible water geyser outside the kitchens bay window. I hear glass crack from somewhere deep within the home. The noise is deafening. They say it sounds like a freight train. Whomever "they" are, they are right. I fall to my hands and knees telling the kids to get down. Scrambling over to my side, together we ride out the rolling jolts as things fall off shelves; cabinets open spilling their contents and small fissures continue to appear in the walls around us. Finally, as the first round of the earth moving seems to subside, I grab my phone from my back pocket hitting the smiling face of my husband to dial him. It goes straight to voice mail. The kids and I stand up gently so as to avoid the broken glasses and dishes. I loved that set of stone ware dishes.

Trying to dial Josh again yields virtually the same results, only this time the three tones answer my call followed by the automated voice.... *we're sorry but your call can't go through. Please hang up......* I hang up before the message is finished.

Looking out the now splintered bay window, the entire row of tightly fitted homes on the other side of the street is gone. Just gone. Even through the white cloud and I can see the rubble begins at about the fourth or fifth step that used to be a landing to each entry way. Water is still spewing from several broken lines, and there is a hissing, as if from a gas line. The white cloud of what I can only presume to be plaster just hangs ominously in the now still air.

Out of habit I check my phone again. Still no service. Still no word from Joshua.

"Mom, what's happening?" Sheila, my oldest, who just last year became a teenager asks of me. A bright and happy girl with a quick wit and a whole lot of ambition. Her brother by comparison is usually quiet and shy.

Jason looks over at her as if she has three eyes "It's an earthquake stupid." He says.

"Don't call your sister stupid." I automatically jump in. "Go to your rooms, we're not going anywhere today. Not until we talk to your father." Both kids race to their rooms, happy to have a break from that place of torture and education.

Walking around the house, looking at all the obvious damage, I am not surprised by the wall cracks and broken "stuff". Grateful that seems to be the worst of it. What happened to the people across the street? Surely most of them were gone already to work. Our neighbors, the Lims, both leave early for work taking their newborn to the daycare right around the corner. I hope they weren't home. The old lady, Mrs. Whatever her name is, lives all by herself two doors down from the Lims. She's lived here her whole life but I know her kids want to move her to an old folk's home and sell the pretty little one bedroom one bath. I guess they won't have to worry about that now.

Looking out the window again, I can't wrap my head around what's happened. Standing there shaking, thinking that could have been us What if we had lived on that side?

My hands are trembling badly right now while tears drip down my cheeks. I turn on the tap for a drink of water which only sputters out a few dribbles then I hear the knocking of air in the pipes. Staring at it I panic. There's no water in the house. And we have gas lines. I race from the house to the laundry in the garage, downstairs. Everything looks tight. A few fissures in the walls and one long one in the ceiling but otherwise to my eye we're good. Whew. I hit the button to open the garage door, nothing happens. Okay, okay calm down. Josh told me how to do this. Fumbling my way deeper into the garage I reach over the hood of Joshua's green baby. His old fixed up Tracker outfitted with Kevlar wheels and reinforced glass. Grasping, I find the little orange pull tab hanging from above and give it a tug. A metallic snap is my reward and I can now push the door up. Never thought of myself as claustrophobic but somehow, I find relief in knowing I'm not trapped. However the relief is short lived because with the door up, I can now see the devastation firsthand, up close and personal. The sounds are so much louder on the street. The cloud of dust so much thicker. I start to cough while the knot in my stomach threatens to become a pile of breakfast on the floor. *No one still in there got out,* I think. I close my eyes and just try to breath.

Pulling my phone out again does nothing to alleviate my panic, still no bars. There's no traffic noise but several car alarms are incessantly blaring away. I can see one person lying down on the walkway about a half a block away. Do I dare go check on them? No dogs barking giving the outside and eerie silence of a sort with no traffic noise or people that isn't silence at all. The water geyser shooting out from under the broken street about 100 yards away slaps the roadway in a rhythmic nature. The heavy silence that isn't, is unnerving me and I close the garage door again, securing it. My favorite poet in college was Marianne Moore whom I remember said "The deepest feeling always shows itself in silence." And I am terrified. Returning upstairs to my mostly intact home, I try turning the television on, but our old fashioned in-ground cable seems to have been affected as well. Sheila and Jason are now sitting in the living room playing their hand-held games but I can tell they are as nervous as I am.

Sheila asks quietly "When's dad getting home?" eyes still on her game.

"I don't know honey. You know officers are the first responders in these kinds of situations. He may be a while."

The day wears on into dusk. With no power and no running water, lunch is the sandwiches I had made this morning, along with some crackers from the cupboard. I remember we aren't supposed to open the refrigerator so we make some cool-aide from the corner water dispenser. Josh always insisted we have it. I thought it was a silly expense, but right now I'm very glad.

Night is coming on, the temperature dips and a damp creeps in since there has still been no power. In fact, there's been no nothing! No officers, no repair crews, no sirens. The continuing silence has been minimized with the kids normal fighting and fussing at one another only made worse by nervous energy. But it's getting dark and Josh hasn't come home. I saw our next-door neighbor step outside a little while ago but I don't know what for. He's still bumping around his little back yard doing who knows what. I almost went over to talk to him but I don't know him very well. He hasn't turned on any lights, flashlights or candles and doesn't seem to be moving with a purpose in the twilight so I only continue to stare out our garden window.

The electronic toys and tablets have finally run out of juice so the kids are almost, but not quite fighting. I've spent my day being busy, changing the sheets on the beds and picking up the debris of my kitchen. I really did like those plates.

Looking out the now fractured living room window, gives me a clear view of my neighbor's yards. I always keep the sheer curtains pulled to give them and us some measure of privacy. For years I have loved the last twinkle of light they allow into the home but looking out them now, all I can see is our neighbor still in his backyard walking around as if in a daze. Bumping into his own fencing and knocking over his lawn furniture. He looks drunk. Sheila comes over to me at the window and says "Mr. Anderson is one of them now isn't he." There's a finality to her sentence which really isn't a question but more a statement of fact.

"One of whom honey?" I ask, not taking my eyes off the odd scene even knowing how rude it is to watch a neighbor in their own back yard.

'Those Myrna things. The dead... zombies." She whispers quietly.

"I am sure you are not allowed to call them that at school and I don't want you to think it's okay now." I respond more out of habit.

Whispering, Sheila looks at me with red rimmed eyes getting ready to cry "I think this is it. I think this is what dad told us about and practiced with us for."

I look at my very much grown-up daughter who is standing beside me quaking in fear. Having just turned fourteen she seems both incredibly grown up and very very young. Crushing her to me in a hug I need as much as to reassure her as myself we just stand watching Mr. Anderson look like a slow but loose human pin ball in his own back yard.

Growing up, Josh had taken our daughter and her brother camping once a year every year since they were little. He would take the SUV in the garage, pack it and them up and go practice "prepping" as he called. It gave me some wonderful me-time to myself so I never questioned it. I never believed in all his doomsday world-ending nonsense. I let him have his little delusions. But now, I have to wonder if maybe he was right. The sunlight is just about gone and it will be completely dark soon. The air is rapidly cooling down as it is known to do in the damp San Francisco weather.

Releasing us both from the embrace I tell her "Come away from the window, we've been rude long enough." Sheila does as she is told without an argument. During a more normal moment in time, I might be amazed at that fact alone. Right now, my brain doesn't even really register it. Jason is now fussing about how none of his games work and because there are no bars on his phone he can't even talk to his friends. Freed of the awkward embrace Sheila huddles with Jason on the couch and they whisper con-spiratorially. I take a seat on the loveseat, not sure what more I can do but wait for the encroaching darkness. Josh still isn't home and it's time by my phone's display, for him to start yet another shift.

As if on cue, hopping up from their seats, my two children hurry off to their rooms returning with their prepacked backpacks their dad has them make up and adjust every year. Changing out clothes the that no longer fit, updating technology and other things I don't remember, was always a part of their ritual. They drop them in the middle of the floor and Sheila goes to our room returning with the backpacks for myself and their dad, adding them to the pile. Jason picks them up together and struggling under the weight, heads downstairs to the laundry dragging his load behind him. Sheila enters the kitchen. I can hear her rummaging around, opening cabinets and drawers. She returns shortly with two of the reusable grocery sacks over filled with what looks to be everything in my pantry. She drops them in the now empty middle of the living room floor. Looking around the house, she lowers her voice "Mom. I need you to listen. Dad told us this could happen. Well that something could happen. Where does he keep his gun?"

"I don't think that is any of your business." I reply swiftly. Sheila sighs while rolling her eyes. Josh's sister Ellan used to do this. I hated it then from her and I hate seeing it now in my own child.

Jason comes stomping back up from the lower level saying "Everything's been stowed, water's been added. Should we leave now or wait until morning?" Glancing around, he sees Sheila and I having a bit of a standoff. Grabbing the two grocery sacks he traipses back downstairs with them, questions left unanswered.

Sheila asks again "Mom, this is important. Where does dad keep his gun?" Inadvertently my eyes flick to the wooden shelf with our family photos on it. Sheila follows my eyes, sighing and starts pushing and poking at the underside of the shelf.

"It's on the side." I say quietly. She finds the concealed release and the bottom of the shelf slides silently open revealing a single pistol snugged securely, held in place by its custom foam insert. Also safely ensconced is an additional pair of loaded magazines. Josh would try and try to get me to go to the range to practice but I was always too nervous. I would just sit and watch him teach the kids how to safely shoot. Now, I watch my daughter take the weapon and its spare parts and go downstairs. I return the shelf to its former state.

I don't like guns. I've lived my whole life in California and never needed a weapon like that. Maybe pepper spray a time or two, but not a gun. Standing by the shelf I look around the house, our home for the last fifteen years. Josh should be home soon. They can't make him work more than twenty-four hours even in an emergency. The union said so. Both kids come clomping up the stairs and veer off to their rooms but neither close the doors.

Looking out my front window I can see things moving in the dark. Human things. I had thought at first looters. You always see pictures of the people breaking in and stealing things on the news after natural disasters. Maybe we would need that gun after all. I have to keep my children safe. But these people in their torn clothes aren't carrying cell phones or crow bars or other weapons and seem to wander aimlessly; actually bumping into inanimate objects like giant pin balls. What few cars that were parked on our side of the street, get their alarms set off from time to time by these people. I don't understand it. Why does no one come out to turn off their alarms, or yell at the people colliding with their cars.

"No one's left mom. We have to leave in the morning. These zombies," she indicates with a wave of her hand "are all that's left." I hadn't heard Sheila come up behind me.

"Of course they aren't honey," I reply. But I am beginning to wonder.

"Mom, dad always taught us if we have to get out," She pauses, "really get out, we are to go to Aunt Ellan's house. In Arizona."

"Your Aunt Ellan is dead." I remind her.

"You know what I mean. Uncle Liam, with cousins Patrick and Jack. That they would take us in." She is speaking softly, as if not wanting to draw the creatures outside attention. Yes, I know what she means. Josh made me promise to do just that, should as he says, the shit hit the fan. He said it had been all prearranged. Money, paperwork, identifications everything.

I watch a woman bounce off a darkened light pole only to become so enraged she attacks the pole grabbing at it, biting it trying to destroy it with her bare hands. This seems to draw the attention of some others, who in turn mimic her madness. That's what this has to be, some kind of temporary madness. The alternative is too horrible to contemplate.

Now at least six people are attacking this light pole. I don't understand it. I hear a whirring noise from the living room that I recognize as our small hand crank radio. Jason used to love turning the hand crank as fast as he could when he was little. Now he stops and tries tuning it,I presume for music but instead he stops at a news broadcast:

This is the emergency broadcast alert system for the greater Combined Bay area. The Myrna reservoir has been breached.

Over a million active Myrnas have been released into the city. All city services are stopped.

No fire response, no police response. Government officials urge all remaining citizens to shelter in

place if safe or flee if they can. There is no estimated time for repairs or aid.

I repeat all city services are stopped. This message will repeat with updates as they become available.

Jason looks at Sheila with a wide-eyed stare that I catch myself imitating as well. Sheila closes her eyes and seems to gather her thoughts. She's just a child. How is it I am looking to her for answers. Opening her eyes, she proclaims "Let's take the mattresses downstairs and sleep in the garage. We can lock the fire door between the house and us. Dad said we can pee in the utility sink down there if we have to. The rest of the supplies are in the car. We'll be safe there until morning, when there's light. "Jason hops to his feet and heads into my bedroom. I can hear him tugging at our large queen mattress. I always wanted a king size bed but it just wouldn't fit into our little home. Mechanically, I follow suit. Together we three drag the heavy mattress, along with pillows and blankets down the narrow stairs to the landing that serves as afire barrier between the garage slash utility room and the remainder of the house to settle in for the night.

Waking up before the kids is normal in my routine and I can tell by the light peeking in from the corners of the aluminum garage door it's pretty early still. It doesn't help that I don't think I actually slept last night between the ground still shaking and rolling; the walls and pipes creaking and cracking and the terror of it all. Around two a.m. I finally noticed how quiet it was. Why didn't the siren's come on? What happened to the sirens? We had always been told if a real emergency were to happen the sirens would sound, so surely it mustn't be that bad, right?

I glance up, distracted from my thoughts, because there's a bumping and thumping coming from above. It has to be Josh, finally home. I practically faint with relief. Now things can get back to normal. Getting up, I go to unlock the deadbolt of the fire door when I hear the kids stir behind me. Sheila races up, slamming her shoulder into the door and ripping the lock from my grip re-securing it.

"No mom. We don't know who's up there." She says flushed and panting.

"It could be your father!" I chastise her desperate to believe it myself.

"No, it couldn't." She says more patiently than I would have imagined. Talking to me as if I am the child and she the adult. "He would have identified himself if it was." I slump against the door, knowing what she is saying to be true.

Apparently, whoever was upstairs has now come down the short flight of stairs and is bumping around outside of the door. Not really knocking and not trying the knob. Just making noise on the other side. My last hope becomes dashed as I realize and accept what is really outside that door. No, Joshua would never have not let us know he was home. This isn't Joshua. A new cold fear grips me.

Jason is loading the pillows and blankets into the car without saying a word. His brows are furrowed and he's making every attempt to be as quiet as possible. He's so small. His short steps and hunched mannerisms make him seem even smaller and younger in my eyes. My stomach knots even tighter as I realize I left my purse upstairs last night. My purse, which has my car keys in it. "Sheila," I stammer "I don't have the keys. They are in my purse."

"I got your purse last night mom." Jason says from the back seat of the car, yawning and stretching. Getting back out, he goes to relieve himself in the square utility sink in the corner of the garage. We turn our heads busying ourselves with, I don't know what. How can I drive this vehicle to Arizona by myself? I hardly ever drive any more. Public transportation is so much easier and cheaper. Maybe we should try to get another broadcast? Josh has never not come home. The kids need breakfast, but there's someone in our home, outside this very door. Oh my god, there's someone outside that door. My quick intake of breath causes Sheila to glance at me. She's on the ground peering out the crack in the garage's door. She puts her finger up to her lips shushing me. "There's a bunch of them out there. More than last night. We are going to have to make a break for it, mom."

"What? What are you talking about?"I ask. Following her lead, I too am whispering though I really don't know why.

She scoots over and motions me to join her on the floor."There's a bunch of them now just walking around but once we open the door it will attract them and we'll have to move fast."

"A bunch of who? What are you talking about?"I am still confused by all of this, my brain refusing to grasp at the straws. Are we really talking about abandoning our home? And how are we supposed to leave without their dad? But when I get down on all fours and lean further down to peer out the small crack, I can see the street is practically a Mardi Gras of the Myrna's. My bile rises. I really need my morning coffee-house stop. Jason brings a paper map showing a route highlighted from our home all the way to Arizona. I presume to Josh's dead sister's house. Ellan's house. She and I never got along all that well to begin with. First when she was turned into a werewolf, then she actually I don't know killed? Ate? Mauled? Her husband and turned him into one. What a freak show. Then right before she died, both of her children were turned into monsters too. Joshua said she didn't do it herself, but heck why not. They were all headed down that path after all. I always felt that the only reason Joshua was a cop at all, instead of having a higher paying job he was qualified for, was because she had been one. He idolized her, as most little brothers do their older big sisters.

Jason is still shoving the map under my nose whispering about routes and travel and getting there. Closing my eyes, I push myself up to my feet. Just standing again seems to help my resolve, and I brush my knees off giving me time to regain my thoughts.

"Mom, mom listen to me." Sheila whispers. "You and Jason get in the car. I'll pop the garage door and throw it open then get in shotgun. Once I'm in, you go. You don't stop for anyone or anything in your way. You just go out the garage, down our little street to Flower. You turn onto Flower then onto the freeway. Get us to the freeway she repeats then asks "Can you do that?" looking at me apprehensively. I nod my head, thinking of course I can drive to the freeway. Jason has stopped shoving the map at me and gotten into the SUV gently closing the door. So unlike his normal noise that travels with him everywhere he goes.

I find myself following my daughters' instructions, buckling myself into the driver's seat. Both of my children cringe slightly when I, out of habit, slam the door shut. Sheila reaches over the hood of the SUV tugging sharply on the orange pull chord exactly as I had done last night. The metal door gives a slight pop and jumps up an inch or two now released of its tension lock. Bending down she takes a deep breath, throws it all the way open and runs back into the passenger side seat slamming her door yelling "go, go go" to me. Light floods the garage and I lurch the vehicle out of it's parking space. Joshua always backed it in for an easier exit. He said it was safer that way. As I exit the short driveway, several of these dead people come into my path and I slow so as not to hit them. What are they doing? Get out of the way!

But they aren't really people, not anymore. I have to keep thinking this way or I don't think I can do this. One has an open gash that somehow is no longer bleeding from his collar bone to his groin with.... parts.... leaking out. Another's head is almost a complete 180 but still somehow sitting on his shoulders. Some others are missing limbs altogether and all are slowly advancing on us in stumbling tripping steps. I press the accelerator squishing my eyes almost completely closed while turning my head. This can't be real. Sheila is still chanting, almost under her breath "go, go go."

The vehicle lurches down the drive and I manage to turn it onto our street only grazing our mailbox while knocking a few of the closer zombie people things over. Turning onto Flower Street half a block down, I see dozens and dozens more of these dead not dead Myrnas all over the place. That's what they have to be my mind says, but I don't understand how. The government said they contained them all. Something must have gone wrong. Oh God, I think. Joshua. He could be out here in this. But my daughter is still chanting at me at each turn, guiding me thru the directions predetermined on the map. I slowdown to avoid running over a man who has no pants on and who seems to be holding his phone with his right hand while waving a coffee carafe in the other. Sheila's quiet chant becomes a louder frantic "Go mom, just go".

I accelerate onto the freeway on-ramp which is eerily empty as we travel east on our journey of ... escape? ... running? ...to whatever this is I don't know and our journey begins.

Liam, A Years' Loss

I miss coffee. The smell of every morning's coffee would overwhelm my senses and fill the house before I ever woke up. My wife and mate Ellan made coffee every morning, drinking it off and on all day long. It was so intermixed with her scent as to be a part of her. It's been a year and no one's made coffee in the house. What an odd thought, as I lay in the not quite shadow of a deep sage bush watching a pair of mourning doves make their nest close by, my grizzled muzzle resting on my front paws. They are apparently oblivious to my presence. I am mostly immobile. It is comfortably cool this early in the morning before the light really has a chance to take hold and I find myself drifting in and out of sleep again. I stay wolf more than human these days, ever since my mate died. My light grays and tans allow me to disappear in a way I can't manage in reality.

It's been a little over a year since she died. It's my fault. She had come to rescue me from an A-mpd Myrna that had me trapped on a hotel rooftop like some damsel in distress. That should have been my job. But somehow it always fell to Ellan. She was the more dominant of us and being younger she was generally stronger and certainly faster than me. We had just gotten done holding a group of degenerate wolves who had taken up cage fighting by drugging up zombies, called Myrnas, against kidnapped werewolves.

Mark and the Phoenix Pack had asked for our help in rounding them up. Ellan could never resist helping if the cause was a moral one. We had gone in and I guess you could say pacified the wolves for the pack to take control over. Ellan was so dominant that I had never seen anyone succeed in fighting against her compulsion. She could stop an entire pack of wolves in their tracks, making them immobile with only the force of her will. Her dominance. Yet despite that, she never saw our pairing as unbalanced or unequal. I know she loved me deeply and I guess I never realized how utterly and completely I loved her.

Ever since that day and her sacrifice, I can't stand to be human. In my human form, every time I close my eyes, I see the nightmare again and again of watching her grab that zombie by the throat and take it, sailing over the edge of the building, with her. I wake up panting, sweating and shaking; my heart racing.

Prior to being turned, I had already had several small heart attacks and strokes. Modern medicine had given up on me and my only option was to be placed in hospice. But Ellan wouldn't give up on me. She changed me at the very moment of what should have been my death. Refusing to give up on me, she changed me. Gave me a new lease on life and I killed her. Or at the very least I watched her kill herself for me. Thinking about it now brings an involuntary whine from my throat.

It's not like I don't go home from time to time. Of course I do. I go home, check on our sons and the pack every so often. In that same set of altercations the local pack's Alpha, Mark had been killed as well. Once Jack, my youngest had fully claimed control of the pack, his strength and force of will have allowed the lesser wolves; and they were all lesser wolves to him; to no longer feel the need to fight everyone that came along. His calm gave protection to the lowest ranking wolves and his dominance gave order to the others. Tensions had been slowly shifting in a downward and positive way. The new pack structure and rules have made for a few tense situations, but things are smoothing out. Jack was just as dominant as Ellan ever was. I fear for him. Werewolves rarely live long in our world.

For me however, interacting as human was still difficult. It was my fault and I knew it. I couldn't bear to look into our sons' eyes. Neither boy, nor anyone in the pack blamed me for her death. Some even said she was so badly wounded fighting the Myrna's that she was a walking dead wolf and she did everyone a favor by taking herself out of the equation. But they should. Blame me that is. The fact that everyone believed it had been her choice and find me without fault only make my guilt that much worse. It's this stink of guilt I can't quite wash myself of.

During the fight with the A-mpd up Myrna zombies she had killed so many of them; but was herself severely bitten and torn by several of them as well. She must have known she had limited time to function before the virus took over and that fact made her probably the single most deadly creature around.

Even grievously and repeatedly bitten, she had come and saved me. She always saved me. I had been cornered on the roof of the hotel and had been using the pool to keep the undead things distanced. I knew that couldn't last forever. I had used all of my energy and strength killing them and getting up to the rooftop while defending the idiot patrons who for some reason, couldn't figure out to stay in their rooms rather than volunteering to become zombie snacks.

Then suddenly there she was. She had burst through the swinging door, leaping over the short gate and gripped and shaken the first of the remaining zombies. It had crumpled to the cool decking like so much garbage finally dead before it had even hit the ground. Ellan had immediately launched herself at the last Myrna. This one had made it around the pool and was within feet of me because I had frozen when I realized she had entered the rooftop pool area. She was supposed to have been in the garage two blocks over helping the Phoenix Pack clear the zombies there and round up the deviant wolves. How she had known I was trapped and in trouble I still don't understand, but there she was. And because I froze, because I looked her way rather than paying attention to the remaining shrieking Myrna, I had allowed that thing to get around the edge of the pool and to close in on me. To immobilize me so I could no longer effectively dodge or run.

I had long since lost my trusty knife and didn't have any other weapons in my hands. And changing takes a really long time. Even though a wolf in human guise, I was still old. Older and more frail than I cared to admit most days and I had pushed myself hard to get that far through several of them.

I watched as Ellan had launched herself across the short corner of the pool grabbing the dead by the throat. But all I could do was watch. She sailed over the short four-foot railing taking her flailing still snapping and grasping zombie with her. Maybe she didn't realize that the railing wouldn't stop her, but I felt she did. It took only a brief span of seconds for her and her prey to fall locked together the four stories to the ground below with a sickening thud.

Every time I close my eyes, I can see that scene as clearly as if it were happening today. Hear the sound of their bodies. The wolf is better at dealing with the pain of the loss and the knowledge that I have to go on. My human heart is sick with grief even now almost a year later.

So, coward that I am, most days I just run on four feet. I enjoy the areas declared as habitat recovery. In the late 2020's Arizona had declared the water crisis beyond critical and moved a significant section of the population out of several high dollar mountainous areas. One of those areas had been the Mountain Ranch homes. The giant man-made lake has been let founder and dry and the homes and business have all been shut down. Even non-indigenous plants were removed.

The area was now considered reclaimed and allowed to nature's own re-growth. Animals freely roam its depopulated homes and forgotten roads. Mountain lions, rabbits, Javelinas, all manner of ground dwelling creatures and especially the birds. All have found a new life in the abandoned acres. Natural ground water was made available to the wildlife through a few cisterns strategically placed and maintained by government workers. But otherwise, it has returned to pristine desert.

It's not off limits per se, it's just most folks don't come up here. It is also understood that emergency services won't come save your dumb ass on a hot day or if you get lost. It is a somewhat popular place to commit suicide and maybe that's what I am doing by hiding up here so often. Waiting, hoping to die.

I lay under this overgrown sage bush dozing secure in the belief of my solitary shade. The ground has a wolf sized depression worn in it from the frequency of my time here. I dream of my dead mate and at times I swear I can still smell her. The oh so distinct musk make its way through my brain to my nose and back into my memories. I dream she is standing over me, protecting me as always.

I hear the pellets rattle through the brush from my side. Very close while simultaneously hearing the shotgun blast. The two young doves I had been enjoying watching are both hit. The male falls where he is, the poor little female remains fluttering about in pain and panic. Her fear and suffering hit me almost instantaneous to the sound. That was damn close and dove season was over last month.

Standing up and whirling around brings a small cloud of dust with it, temporarily obscuring both myself and the shooter. I face the unknown shooter with a snarl on my muzzle; ruff and hackles raised. He is just a few dozen yards downwind and as startled as I. He chose his place well; I didn't smell him. For as much as he startled me, it is clear I in turn scared him, not realizing I was there either. We stare at each other for a moment. Clearly, he's not experienced with wolves. You should never look a pissed wolf in the eye. That's a sure-fire way to get the fight going.

The moment lingers on as we stare at each other him frozen in fear me deciding if I am annoyed and startled enough to attack him. He's a small thing, maybe al of one hundred pounds and young but I find my surprise is nudging into anger, when a warm and firm prod to my shoulder pushes at me, telling me I need to go. This is more than a wisp of my mate's scent. The familiar musk and coffee comes unbidden with the sudden knowledge our oldest son, Patrick is soon to be in trouble. It is time to go. The young man with the shotgun doesn't realize how lucky he is.

I turn, again sending up a small cloud of tan dirt, and dart off in the direction this knowing nudge is giving me. Driving might take me a while between the time to change, the traffic and the roads. But on four feet, traveling is much more a straight line as the crow fly's kind of thing and therefore much shorter. There is an urgency being whispered into my subconscious that I can't otherwise put a finger on. I am wrapped in warmth and a strength, along with the familiar scents of coffee and musk. I speed east, instinctively knowing where I am going. My son, our son, is soon to be in life threatening peril and we have to respond.

Ignoring the Havenot that shot my young doves is probably for the best anyway. They are a sad bunch, eking out a meager living on the outskirts of society. With my turn and sprint in the opposite direction I feel the push sending me, I am quite sure this is a tale the young man will bravely tell of the wolf who turned tail and ran.

Patrick, A New Beginning

Fia raises herself up from the bed, trying her best not to disturb her new mate, Patrick. Pushing the tousled covers aside, she steps lightly and gently to the small trailer's kitchen window. Lifting her chin taking note of the lightening sky an involuntary shiver runs down her spine. Sunrise is mere moments away. The early predawn of February is still cool and she can feel the chill through the thin pane of glass in her compact twenty-two foot home trailer on wheels. She is a part of the Festival Pack. One of only three packs in the entire country permitted to travel freely without fear of retribution. And they are home to the Ye Olde Fair entertainment. A traveling performing group of pseudo-Renaissance performers that is mostly filled with werewolves, their families and the workers who travel with them. Fia is one of the performers and a cousin of some degree more or less to the packs Alpha, Falco.

With the rising sun, Fia's fears return to overpower the odors otherwise permeating the small area of sex, excitement and satisfaction. She can feel the mating tie firmly in place somewhere deep in her, filling a place she had long known was empty. It is warm and strong, vibrant and comforting. She returns to sit on the edge of the bed looking down at him, her new mate. Patrick stirs enough to put a hand over her hips and smile softly, still embedded in the remnants of sex, sleep and the newfound comfort of the shared mating tie.

"Quick, it's almost light. You have to go before Falco finds you here." Fia whispers urgently disturbing his pleasant aura.

"If Falco doesn't already know we are mated, that's his deficiency. No shower will wash our mating tie away." Patrick lifts his head, deeply inhaling the air to let the scent of sex and mating fill him, wiggling his dark eyebrows playfully. "It will be okay, I promise." He takes her hand kissing it gently. Brown eyes meet her even deeper brown ones. Eyes with a hint of copper in them.

Fia gives a soft almost feline purr, her scent slipping back towards musky rather than the earlier fear. Her wolf satisfied with their choice of mate. He is young, strong and brother to the local packs Alpha.

Patrick reaches for his jeans with one hand, while sitting up and pulling her closer to him with his other. His warm scent wraps around them both and calms her a bit, giving her a center she is just now coming to recognize. Standing up, they rise together and get to the task of cleaning up in the trailer's tiny bathroom. Twenty-two feet is not a lot of space and the bathroom isn't much more than a medium closet. While Fia is a small slip of a girl coming to no more than five and a half feet tall, Patrick stands over six feet with broad shoulders.

Outside the day blooms in the Gold Canyon area of Arizona. The rising sun gives its mountains the beautiful majestic yellows and blues. Sounds can be heard from all around Fia's home as the early weekday means no performances or crowds of people. Like an ant colony bustling about, it's just practice for the performers, repairs and restocking for the laborers and typical household chores for the families.

Inhaling once more deeply, Patrick's nose is giving him all the information his ears and eyes can't right now. Not only is Falco outside, but a pair of wolves he's not familiar with as well. Sighing a bit, he knows this can't be put off any longer. For his new mate's sake, he hopes this doesn't turn out to be a fight.

Turning to face his new mate, he gently raises her chin up so as their eyes meet. "Fia, they are here and we are going. Are you sure you are okay with leaving your trailer behind? Because I can have someone come get it. You've lived here a long time."

"No, I just want to be gone. "She can smell the stink of her own fear and rising panic and tries to steady herself by reaching mentally for the new but warmly throbbing mating bond. Her fear could push one or all of the wolves outside to do something she wasn't sure she could live with. She's seen first hand over the years how her pack used intimidation to dominate and control others.

Smiling at her, Patrick takes her hand. He exits the narrow steep trailer steps with her in tow. Outside, there are groupings of travel trailers set up six to a circle; each with a wooden picnic bench, park style barbecue grill and a few folding chairs in the center. While all the other circles of trailers have movement and noise bustling about them, the one Fia's trailer is a part of, is oddly silent. Only the Alpha and his henchmen are in attendance to this showdown today it would seem. But Patrick knows better. He is acutely aware of the ears listening, waiting for the fight that might very well mean his death. And if it comes to that, they will kill their own pack mate as well for daring to leave without the Alpha's approval and permission.

Readily seen are two large wolves sitting beside the central bench on the ground while an older man dressed in work clothes, complete with overalls, steal toed shoes, and a piece of dry grass between his teeth, lounges deceptively on the bench with one foot up on the seat facing them.

Fia's seen this act before. Falco only puts on the I-don't-care act when in fact he is mad enough to kill. Instinct honed by years of subservience in her pack causes her sharp intake of breath and to completely freeze in place waiting for the punishment her body knows is coming. This allows Patrick to let go of her hand while taking another step forward placing himself between her and the not so welcome committee. Being newly mated he can feel her fear, her submission. His mother always taught him; you protect what is yours and she was now his. A snarl begins on his lips he can't quite control.

"We are mated now. There is nothing you can do." Patrick boldly proclaims. The two wolves flanking Falco, though silent, display large white teeth. One snaps his jaw in eager anticipation. Their claws make deep marks in the loose silty dirt. But Falco continues to lean casually on the table as if for all the world this didn't interest him. Seemingly to ignore or misread Patrick's aggressive stance and threatening words.

Placing both feet on the ground with his head still slightly offset he replies softly, "Oh pup, there is always something I can do. But you are correct, you two are mated. I can smell it from here." It's at this point Falco's blue eyes meet Patricks brown ones in a clear attempt of Alpha dominance.

"Fia will come with me to be a part of the Phoenix Pack." Patrick goes on undeterred. His youth giving him a bravado not yet earned. His brain telling him this is not going well, while his animal instincts tell him his mate is being threatened.

"It's not that simple boy. You're so new I can smell the shine and feel the fear. You see Fia is like me. Come out of the womb a wolf, natural-born. And we are a rare species. Not a mutt, bitten in, like you. If you think for one minute I'd let her go, well I guess we'll just have to disabuse you of that notion." As Falco finishes his monologue the two wolves flanking him stand up, swaying back and forth on their front feet. It's easy to read their eager intent. They quiver with expected anticipation. Patrick never takes his eyes off their Alpha.

"Being Festival Pack doesn't change the fact that this is Phoenix Pack territory. Your rights can be revoked."

A third wolf, larger than most and easily a size match for either of Falco's guards arrives with his head lowered. A snarl rippling his muzzle exposing long lethal fangs, stalking slowly around from the back of the trailer. The grizzled muzzle belies the clear and deadly intent. Fia lets out a startled squeak jumping to the side, bumping into Patrick who has not paid any attention to this newcomer as he passes close enough she could reach out and touch him. None of the group had heard or smelled this new intruding wolfs approach.

Still flinching while this new wolf passes, Fia steps into Patrick's space. Patrick never takes his gaze from the Alpha challenging him, nor pays the newcomer any attention, his nose already telling him what he needs to know. This new-to-the-party wolf has his gaze set only on Falco. Fia is certain Patrick is about to be torn to shreds and tries to warn him of the intruder she does not recognize. But this wolf, with his silly splash of white across his face walks up to Patrick's side and takes up the challenge to the Alpha also with a direct stare to the eyes and a further deep rumbling snarl.

Patrick has recognized his father's scent readily enough and so continues to also stare straight at Falco in what most would consider an unwise challenge. Falco is known to not only be many decades or even centuries old but treacherous and deceptive. Lowering his hand to stay the wolf at his side gives acknowledgment to both sides that this wolf is here under Patrick's pack authority. Not knowing how his father knew he was in over his head isn't really his main worry at the moment, but his human brain is grateful for the support and thinks there just might be a way to get out of this alive for all of them.

"I think we will be on our way now. And when someone comes to pick up Fia's belongings which is to include her trailer, I don't expect there to be any trouble or damage. "Patrick turns on his heel effectively dismissing the old Alpha. Taking Fia in hand again he walks them all towards the visitors parking, trusting his father to protect them from any wayward thinking wolves or sneak attacks. The Alpha of the Festival Pack shakes with barely contained rage. His two lower ranking wolves practically attack each other from their unsatisfied pent-up madness and frustration of losing what they had believed was to be easy prey. None of them aware why they didn't kill the insolent youth who just stole one of their pack mates.

"Boy, this is the last time your pack takes something of mine." Falco whispers through his clenched jaw. In anger Falco takes out his frustrations on the two wolves still sitting at his side.

Liam, Call To Action

Hopping into Patrick's truck, well more like clambering for me; we three settle in for the drive home. It's a good long drive and I find the exhaustion to be too much. Once that little push of energy or intent is gone, the adrenaline leaves with it. I am hurting in ways that are concerning, leaving me exhausted and shaky. My heart is racing too hard and my chest is on fire. I know they can hear me wheezing just to breathe. The direction and energy Ellan was sharing with me has gone and with it any enhanced stamina or strength. Somehow, I finally manage to drift off to sleep.

Waiting at the door upon our arrival, even though I don't think anyone actually texted him, is Jack. Though the younger of my children, he is still the Phoenix Packs Alpha and as such his rule is law. But then this is my mate's house, or I guess mine now. So things are never as easy as they should be. I slip past him, not slinking necessarily, but not meeting his eyes. My wolf still feels the need to give way to Jack's dominance where as my human form is more likely to argue. He may be my son who stands easily six foot four but he is Ellan's equal in supremacy of will and I can feel he is revved up for an argument. With Patrick's new mate in tow however, it shouldn't be too bad or so I hope. Thus far none of the fights between the boys have turned physical. I fear that day is yet to come.

Passing through the door and traveling down the hall I find Bethy sitting inside. She looks for all the world as if she was just a large shepherd type dog instead of the deadly werewolf I know her to be. Her red gold coat impeccably in place as always, she whines at me to let me know her sympathies are with me. Ellan had in some odd way adopted her as part of our little tribe even though officially she had become a Phoenix Pack member. I trot the length of the house to the master bedroom that I still occupy, though without my mate it doesn't feel like anything more than a temporary stop. Ellan's clothes still hang in the double walk-in closet; her pillows still adorn the right side of the bed. Even her hairbrush still lies on the antique tallboy dresser she kept. Her scent is everywhere here, though slowly fading. Pushing the door closed with a rear foot, I hop onto our bed, nestle into the rich comforter and settle myself in for a well-deserved second nap. Or maybe it's my third, but who's counting.

***

Placing Fia's hand in his, Patrick helps her out of his old truck and together they walk up the driveway to stand in front of Jack. Their matching brown eyes meet briefly. Taking a deep breath, Jack inhales Fia's scent and recognizes the mating bond that has fallen into place. His brother is now mated. Though not mated himself, his wolf brain knows this fact to be true. Closing his eyes for a moment to inhale again this time more deeply is more for equilibrium than gaining any additional information his nose could share. He clenches a fist momentarily, then the moment passes.

Tipping his head in an inquisitive manner he opens the dance, "Welcome. You are Fia I presume? Patrick has of course, spoken about you." Fia lowers her blue eyes in deference to the Alpha and dips her head in the submission of a uniquely canine fashion. Her graceful neck exposed as only a canine does, to show servility and deference.

"May we come in brother?" Patrick asks cautiously, still keeping his eyes level but averted to over the shoulder. His body positioned still just a step ahead of his hesitant mate.

Turning from the door, Jack steps aside giving acceptance to the pair. As they pass by him, a low rumble is felt through their feet, not quite shaking the ground, but neighboring dogs begin howling and waling while even the feral cats of the neighborhood scatter. The brothers look at one another, all animosity forgotten in the moment and enter the house together. Following the wide-open swath of the room to a computer desk set apart but partially hidden in a small alcove down the west hallway they join forces as they always have, working together. Patrick sits down in front of the keyboard without hesitation, typing in the US Geological website from memory. Jack starts scrolling through feeds to get a clearer picture of what has just happened, while fielding a few stray texts from pack members over the event. Fia is lost to them as their focus has now shifter and not knowing what to do with herself, sits on the oversized sectional in the main room.

Popping up on the screen under event notifications are the bold words Earthquake and California along with a rather large number of 9.2. Further details reveal the entire Pacific Northern Seaboard has been affected.

"Go turn the news station on please." Jack asks of no one in particular, waving his hand in the general direction of the TV in the other room.

Bethy trots into the room as if in answer to his query heading for the TV and easily hits the remote. Fia glances at the new wolf and stiffens. She leans towards the little golden wolf but stops, realizing she is still a guest in this home. Her breath hitches in her breast. Neither of the brothers are paying attention, their focus being on the large nearby earthquake and the rapidly launching news castors' delight in the sharing of mass devastation and destruction. Just how many times one man can say "reports are still coming in" is mind numbing.

"Patrick, please go call the pack. This will have over-reaching consequences, I'm sure." Jack softly asks, still intent on the geological site. "Tell them meeting in three hours, here but not mandatory." Without hesitation at the order Patrick takes out his phone and begins a group text.

Something in the air causes him to look up from his phone while his fingers still fly away in unconscious action. Patrick notices for the first time the tension in the room is due not to the bombardment of bad news, but rather Bethy and Fia staring each other down in a show of shock, surprise and dominance. With his back to his brother, Patrick goes to Fia drawing her in gently to him while steering her away from the room and closing the front door. Her eyes, as big as saucers, dart around once quickly looking for the trap. Resting his hand on her waist "What's wrong? That's our pack mate Bethy." He softly intones. It seems incredible to him that Bethy, the lowest member of the pack, would find it within herself to challenge his new mate and most especially within his own home. He cocks his head at her while frowning as if somehow by vision alone he could figure out what the problem is. The scent is stirring up in the air now, and Jack becomes aware of the situation. Furrowing a brow and giving a similar head tilt, the silent command to Bethy rings in her head "Later."

With that command the little red gold wolf shakes herself from tip of nose to tail and turns, exiting back through the kitchen. Flicking his eyes back to the screen then to Patrick, Jack gives the same light command to him as well.

Obscenely flashing on the screen – the news feed reads:

Massive California Earthquake Kills Thousands. Millions of dead loose. California is closing its borders. Emergency response has been put in place and all air traffic has been halted. It's a strike not seen in a century.

***

Sleep fails to come as my mind races back to earlier this morning when I believed I had smelled the coffee Ellan used to make. Feeling her brush her hands over my coat as she would have, when we were working together was more than a memory. Feeling that mental push she could give when giving me directions. I used to chafe under that at times I'll admit but today I know what I felt. Prior to this morning, I thought she had finally left me. Gone forever. I had felt so abandoned without being able to smell or feel her. I had fallen into a type of melancholy I guess you could say. She's been dead a year now, but somehow feeling her presence gives me a comfort I didn't know I needed. No, that's a lie. I know exactly how much I needed it. So, I had responded eagerly by going and helping my oldest son and his brand-new mate escape to the safety of our home and pack. It felt like old times. Like I had a purpose again. She gave me that. Direction. Thereby breaking my daily routine of sleeping under the brush in the habitat recovery area hoping to fade into nothingness. And before they could even get into the house, we had all felt it. The bone jarring earthquake I knew, instinctively to be trouble. So much for the third nap. Even lying on our bed, trying to rest now, I know I can't. I can hear the boys tippy tapping on the keyboard of the desktop computer. Now the television has been turned on to scroll through news feeds. I sigh and start my change. I need to be human for this. Damn, this is going to hurt. Shifting back to human still takes a good twenty or thirty minutes and leaves me panting and in pain, but I must be human to speak to my sons and formulate a plan. Guess I have a few shifts left in me yet.

Even while changing, my hearing is still better than human. That's how I know Jack has reached into his pants pocket drawing out his phone. His first call is to his Uncle Joshua in San Francisco. Joshua is Ellan's younger brother. He's not, nor can he be, a werewolf having chosen to get serum shots over time but they are family none the less and I know promises were made. Getting no answer, he then tries Joshua's wife Lillith, again getting no response. Lillith and our family never really got on. She was too pretty and too pampered. First by her parents, then by Joshua. But her children are as much pack as my own boys. And we protect pack. The swelling of my desire to protect can only be from the left-over embrace of my dead wife.

My sons have been disagreeing over a plan of action when the packs second and thirds begin calling in. Everyone asking what was being put in the works. Many have extended family in the affected areas. I need to go talk to the packs Alpha who is my son, Jack. I could hear, even in the middle of changing, that they still couldn't reach Ellan's brother or our sister-in-law after several attempts. We need to go find them, bring them here, to safety. I should by all rights tell him what I plan to do but there it is again, that subtle push. That waft of coffee and musk and scent that is or rather was my mate and wife. I hesitate with my hand on the bedroom doorknob.... Wait it tells me. What am I going to tell him? Ask his permission? Wait to see what he says? The push wraps itself around me allowing me to believe it's command as it grows, to become stronger, more urgent, insistent even. So wait I will. In the mean time I suppose it would be best if I actually got showered and dressed before going out there in any case. Wouldn't want to scare the natives.

A few minutes later and that quick shower done, I feel a bit more myself. Just myself with no traces of that other worldly presence. Sometimes I think I must be losing my mind. A knock at the door startles me out of my preoccupied state of looking for clean pants. Opening the door, Jack's pursed lips tell me he is aware of some of what I was thinking and feeling.

"Dad, whatever you are thinking of doing, don't. We need you here right now." He takes a deep breath as if testing the air and frowns slightly. Surely he can't smell his mother beyond the usual. Her clothes still populate our walk-in closet. My son Jack has ascended, which is the only way of putting it, to being Alpha of the Phoenix Pack by virtue of being the single most dominant wolf in the territory and surrounding environs. But for all of that, Jack is still only nineteen and feeling his way around. My late wife Ellan should have been the packs Alpha but loathed the responsibility so he's had an incredibly steep learning curve. Being that Ellan had spent her life and her career as a law enforcement official; she didn't crave any more of that responsibility as a wolf. Ellan only became a wolf shortly after our first son Patrick's birth due to what should have been a deadly car accident.

Mark was an Arizona native but had become the Phoenix Pack's Alpha then forming a tight, close knit functional group. But wolves are creatures of dominance and structure and as such, he often looked to Ellan, and myself more by default, to help guide him in his decisions. One of those had been the creation of the Werewolf Assistance Act. We get to kill these loose dead Myrna turned zombies, thereby not risking human lives and at the same time get paid per bounty. There's a lot more to it, but that was the central piece of legislation enacted.

Jack places his hand over mine which is still holding onto the door knob absently. "Dad, we can't get a hold of Joshua or his family. We need to wait a bit and find out what is going on before going off and doing something rash. In addition, I have called a pack meeting in a couple more hours here at the house and I need you to attend. It would reflect poorly if you weren't here and I need your guidance." When did my son get so wise?

"Sure kiddo. I'm too old to go running off to anyone's rescue." I say with a slight upward twist of the lip in what I hope is an obviously self-depreciating smirk. The crease in his brow deepens briefly, but he lets it go, returning to the front rooms. Werewolves by their very nature are preparers. Preppers as some call them. They protect their families which in human form almost always means stocking piling, preparing and practicing. In wolf form it is all a bit more basic. We eat fight love and protect what is ours. Sometimes the order gets a bit muddled and the what and who to protect can change and shift but it's all basically the same.

Pack Meeting Interruptus

Bringing a bunch of werewolves together can be a tricky thing. Jack made the decision to call the pack to the house, giving the order to Patrick to carry out. Most of the wolves in the pack understood without too much grumbling that this was often a more expedient way to go about things. Truthfully the packs second should have been the one to have made the call, but Joseph is not a vain or arrogant man. His naturally gentle nature allows him to give leeway to things in the Phoenix Pack that would cause fights to the death in other less stable ones. Allowing Patrick to make the communications between the members via link or cell is one of those things that allows the pack to function more smoothly as a cohesive unit. However, even Joseph's good nature only allowed things to go so far. So, he arrived only thirty minutes after the call to come had rung out.

Parking his older Ford truck on the side of the house with the double wide gate as is his habit, Joseph strolls casually through the front door going straight to his Alpha. As foreman of a work crew, he was fortunate to have the flexibility to leave job sites with very little explanation or notice. This often worked well being Second in the Phoenix Pack. At least in this last year with as many changes as had taken place.

When the Alpha Mark died along with a few others, there was quite a bit of scrambling among certain pack members for dominance and higher status. Little did anyone at that time know, Jack was probably the single most dominant wolf on the entire continent who only had to have the push of losing both his mother and Alpha on the same day to allow his power to come forward. Most of the pack had liked and respected not only their Alpha but Ellan and her husband and the rest of the family as well. It was well known Mark himself had changed and trained both her boys. So with limited grumbling and only one serious threat to the safety and harmony of the pack easily eliminated, life for the majority of the pack went on as usual. Most wolves didn't care who was in charge so long as they could live their day-to-day lives with their families, earn a living killing zombies and staying out of the politics of the matter. Neither did Joseph really, especially as he liked both the boys and their dad and so far, things had run fairly smoothly. Status quo seemed like a good plan for all concerned. Entering the home unbidden, Joseph's boots make little sound on the floor but Jack looked up from his computer none the less. Giving him a slight side smile, he resumed his keyboard strokes.

"Hey," Joseph says more to the room than to any one individual, nodding his head at them. Taking note of the strange female wolf sitting awkwardly on the couch with her knees pulled up looking ready to bolt at a moment's notice, he takes a deeper breath. Okay, one of Falco's pack? What's the deal with that? The fear radiating off her could have sent a lower ranking wolf into a protect or be protected mode, but Joseph had lived a fair share of years around many dominant wolves and as such this didn't bother him too much more than mild curiosity. Keeping his eyes level so as not to meet anyone's, he leans casually against the wall while tucking his hands safely in his pockets. While his wolf brain is telling him something more than just an earthquake is up, he isn't feeling the need to be about the place with concern right at this moment either.

Patrick enters the room from the depths of the kitchen carrying some water bottles and a tray of hams and salami. Setting them on the coffee table he nods in greeting to Joseph. "Massive earthquake in Northern California," he says as if Joseph hadn't gotten the pack text or listened to the breaking news gleefully telling of the mass destruction and loss of life on the radio when coming over. More alarmingly was the breach of the Northern Stations Containment Unit. This facility was a hold-over from a previous administration where, quite literally, close to a million zombies were warehoused. It was done in the early phase of the outbreak when a large faction, convinced that a cure could still be found, managed to put political pressure on the Fed's to not destroy their loved ones. Snorting involuntarily, Joseph tries to cover it with a light cough. Patrick has failed to notice as his receding back returns to the kitchen, supposedly to retrieve a second tray of meats. It is always best when gathering a pack of wolves together to have plenty of food available.

Patrick comes from a side hallway this time, nodding in way of greeting as if remembering his wolf manners, allowing Joseph to follow him into the kitchen of the old ranch house. Feeling comfortable is the mark of contentment within any pack and as such Joseph helps himself to a can of soda before opening the conversation. "Who's the girl?" He asks. His body language allows him to lean casually on the black and grey slate countertop with one hip but Patrick, still with his back to him, stiffens. Rummaging through the commercial grade refrigerator for yet another slab of meat Patrick responds "That is Fia. My mate."

Turning to face Joseph the two wolves stare at one another. Not a safe game to play. Joseph's shorter but svelte figure belies an old wolf. Most wolves don't make it past their first fifty years or so. Joseph however is working towards his second century, as well as being second in the pack. While Patrick easily stands a head taller at over six foot and is built more along the lines of football player, his wolf understands that this isn't a dominance play, nor a play for his mate. Still, he must make it understood he will not back down. Thankfully the two wolves seem to come to an unspoken agreement and each resumes his former task with little more than an eye brow raised and clearing of throats.

"You realize Falco will not let another of his pack go without a fight." Joseph says more into the can of carbonated beverage than to Patrick himself. Pausing his refrigerator raid, this time giving Joseph a quizzical look, Patrick asks with his raised eyebrow expression what the old wolf means. "I guess you didn't know Bethy was originally from his pack. She was being sent to a friend of his he owed in payment as a breeder when she ran. And ran straight into your mom." A smirk turns the corners of his mouth up but he takes a deep drink of the soda to cover it. "He barely let that one go without a fight or so I heard," Pausing to emphasize "Ellan somehow persuaded him to drop the matter."

A deep growl breaks the story. Neither man had seen or heard the pretty red gold wolf they had been discussing, Bethy, pad into the room. With her hackles up and her head lowered she is clearly challenging Joseph, whether to say no more or for simply telling her tale neither can be sure. Padding on through to the front room, Bethy snaps her jaws at both of them passing by. Joseph mouths the word "sorry" at her while Patrick looks more befuddled than before.

With the moment passed, Joseph pushes himself off the counter to be able to answer a work text. Patrick shakes his head and resumes his way to the front room with his second tray of protein. Slowly the pack filters in by ones and twos as the time for the meeting draws near. Each member takes a position within the room relative to their position in the pack. Higher ranking members tend to sit in the chairs and on the couch while lower ones lean on the walls and the very lowest seat themselves on the floor with their backs against the wall. Joseph looks around thinking "Maybe this isn't as settled as I'd like to think." Fia has managed to fit herself into a small corner between the couch and a freestanding lamp and like the other lower ranking wolves, keeps her back to the wall.

At the appointed hour Jack stops his typing and texting and straightens himself up, looking around the room as if seeing it population explosion for the first time. Placing his link on mute and setting it on the electronics table he moves to the front of the room, ostensibly in front of the oversized eighty-five inch television taking up the vast majority of one wall. He takes stock of who is and who is not in attendance as well taking note of how everyone has arranged themselves with a sweep of his eyes; a single inhale of scent.

"Welcome friends," he opens with. "As I am sure you are all aware, approximately three hours ago an aggressively large earthquake has hit the San Francisco Greater Combined Bay Area. Many are dead, many more are missing. And the worst of it, is the Containment Area has breached." A few of the more aggressive hunters lean forward with a gleam in their eye, anticipating a large payday with so many zombies involved. Continuing "We do not have any type of contract in the state of California, nor does any other pack." As a wolf named Jim gathers breath to speak Patrick cuts him off and continues "However! That being said, the Vegas and Reno packs both have asked for our help and reinforcement to meet the threat of wandering zombies into their state and territories. Both of these packs have current contracts with their state to destroy zombies just as we do." Taking a breath Patrick reads the room in scent from eager anticipation, to despair to impartial concern. "I have been asked by both Alphas for support. At this time, I will take two pairs of volunteers to travel safely and with permission into the allotted territories to assist with additional kills as needed. You will of course be compensated at that states contractual rate."

Jim leans forward and interjects quickly "I'll go. I volunteer." Nodding in acknowledgement, Patrick continues "Thank you." Returning his attention back to the majority of the room "Please note, at no time under no circumstance are you to enter into the state of California. I know some of you may have relatives and loved ones there." Pausing, Patrick turns his head to the front yard facing large picture window.

An immense dust cloud can be readily seen in a determined path towards the ranch house. A group of rapidly approaching cars engines interrupts the Alpha and soon draws everyone else's attention to that forward-facing window. In short time five cars swiftly pull up and spew forth their passengers. Some in wolf form, some in human but all werewolves none-the-less. Falco walks with determined heavy steps towards the door but falters when his senses catch up to the blinding rage he has worked himself into. He seems to realize there is much more of the Phoenix Pack here than he most likely anticipated. What he had originally envisioned as a simple killing of two young wolves and bringing Fia back by force has now turned into a spectacle he's not quite sure how to deal with.

Shouting from halfway down the drive the old gray-haired Alpha threatens "Get out here you mangy half bitten cur!"

There is some power and command push in that voice letting all the werewolves in the vicinity know he feels he is taking charge. Drawing a deep breath Falco continues, "Return what is mine!" This comes out more roar than words but the meaning is clear to all. Inside the Phoenix Packs meeting, there is confusion, some fear but mostly anger at the obvious threat and insult. The only member of the Phoenix pack in wolf form is Bethy and she is shaking but not from fear, her low rumbling growl can be felt by all the Phoenix pack and adds to the background noise. Patrick lets a roar loose of his own that would do a lion credit and tears the front door open. It swings off its hinges and tilts precariously to one side.

Before he can race through it, a soft but firm command settles in his brain from Jack "Not yet brother." Standing in the doorway Patrick freezes, his breath heaving in both anger and frustration. Jack makes his way to the door, the rest of the pack either taking places to view the encounter from the window or in the case of Joseph and a few others, ready to pile out en masse to the front, to defend their territory.

Jack ducks under Patrick brushing as he goes by. The touch brings the brothers together in a way that allows them to work together drawing strength from one another. Stepping onto the porch Jack appears calm and in control meeting Falco's raging anger with a placid face and steady gaze. Having had a few hours to work himself up into this rage, Falco is barely staying human. His eyes shift from hazel to wolf yellow and back as he speaks. Spittle flies with each word. "Your brother stole what was mine. Your whole pack is nothing but curs and thieves." His wolves advance to form a line with him while his wolves-in-human-shape flank them as if to prevent escape.

Even though young, Jack has been coached in how to deal with threats like this. First in high school as a team leader then as a wolf from the now dead Alpha Mark. "It is time you go," he says. Though his voice is calm there is a deepening; reflecting the growing rage threatening to lose control behind his eyes. "You, your whole pack. We are done here. Your visitation rights are revoked. The Festival Pack is verboten until such time as I and only I allow it." Falco throws his head back and laughs with a power Jack didn't know he had. Fia recognizes this as a classic Falco move to draw attention away from the attack she knows he's just ordered. She can't help but let out a little squeak.

The wolf to Falco's right launches himself at Jack. Barely making a full stride when the sound of a shot rings out. The remaining wolves look around in confusion. Their fallen comrade and pack mates blood splatter out to soak the sparse Arizona grass and dirt, dead before even hitting the ground from the hole in his skull. All eyes quickly find the source of the single lethal shot. Standing behind one of the Phoenix Packs vehicles parked in the driveway is Liam, in human form. Leaning over the hood of the SUV, his finger still on the trigger of the murderous weapon only this time aiming at Falco.

Allowing his rage to overcome his good sense, Falco launches himself at Liam while shifting in mid-air. Changing shape and shedding clothing while moving makes for an incredibly difficult target and Liam misses with his next two shots. One goes wild while the second, though more controlled only manages to graze the enraged Alpha. Finishing his shift, the big white wolf lands on the hood of the vehicle his whole body looking for the target of his fury while roaring his anger and hate in Liam's face. Within that split second of time, both packs rush to the fight when a fourth shot rings out and the white wolf suddenly falls silent. A penetrating wound that was once an eye dribbles blood and viscous fluid, while at its exit point leaves only a remnant where the back of his skull once enclosed his brain. The old wolf tumbles off the car falling with a thud to the ground.

Exploding with equal force but less damage comes the command "STOP" that Jack pushes into everyone's head. All of the werewolves freeze. The Phoenix Pack drops in response to the force of the command, including Liam, causing him to press the side of the black deadly rifle into the ground yet refusing to let go of it. The remaining Festival Packs wolves snort and sneeze while dancing on tip toes trying to find a way to disobey the command forced into their heads by a wolf who was not their Alpha but so dominate that their long lives of utter obedience to the will of a stronger alpha compels them to cease any further actions.

Speaking only in his head so no one else can hear, Jack bids his father to return to the house and to please not shoot anyone else tonight. To his remaining pack members, Jack turns and releases them from their hold telling them to watch and bear witness only. Finally. turning this time to the remaining Festival Pack, Jack says for everyone to hear "It didn't have to go this way. Go home. Take your people and leave. My decree stands, you are forbidden to return and we are done. Anything further and I will order your entire pack wiped from the face of the earth."

A single male, still in human form sidles closer keeping his head turned away from the Alpha that just ordered his packs banishment. Pushing the words out barely above a quivering whisper "Sir, Falco was old. Older than most and a child of the Master Alpha."

Crooking his head in question Jack responds "Does it look like I care?" Sighing, he walks up to the scared and nervous man. Everyone holds their breath, unsure of Jack's intentions. Taking the man's jaw in his hand he turns it to meet his eyes giving the command "Go." Only a little push of his dominant will is needed to induce the man to turn so quickly he trips, falling over his own tangled legs in an attempt to leave. The rest of the remaining Festival's wolves follow with varying degrees of haste and fear.

From the porch, Joseph indicates he's already let The Crow's Nest know about the bodies. When wolves die, they stay in the form they are killed in. Without human bodies, it's a simple matter the governments still aren't sure they want to get involved in and so no official crime is recorded. However, even in wolf form the biometrics of vein pattern recognition still work and can be matched to recorded citizens. The Crow's Nest is the official government agency that bags and tags zombie bodies and ensures that proper payment for any kills is recorded. It's better to be safe and involve them than to explain to a pair of beat cops why the neighbors have the blood and brain goo from two dead bodies in their front yard.

It only takes a few moments for the remainders of the Festival Pack to collect their cars, collect their dead and speed off as fast as they came. Two of the members in wolf form have fled on foot. Jack taking a breath to gather his thoughts gives a small flick of his head, an indicator for Ramon and Isaac to follow ensuring no one decides to sneak back and take revenge. The pair of brothers, though young have become fast friends of both Patrick and Jack. Having been kidnapped; changed against their will, then rescued by Ellan and accepted into the pack, they have a fierce sense of loyalty and are happy to be entrusted with this.

Inside Jack clears his throat, more to gain everyone's eye than to work off nerves. The front door remains hanging oddly and the heat of the Arizona day is working its way through the house now. Somehow he feels calm and assertive even after the not-so-little exchange out front. To rescind a packs permission to travel is not a small thing. Politics in wolves is if anything more complicated and other Alphas are to be at least advised prior to decisions being brought down. Calls will have to be made to ensure support from surrounding packs. No one pack has status over another supposedly, but even so certain formalities must be met or more challenges and deaths will follow. Holding up his hand in a placating gesture he intones "Give me a minute please and we will continue this later." The remaining members take this as their cue to leave and file out. Some fearful while others adrenaline fueled from the almost assault on their pack. Almost everyone is gone leaving only Bethy in her wolf form who essentially lives there anyway, and Joseph as pack second to await what he presumes will be further instructions.

"Joseph. Is there such a thing as a Master Alpha. Do I need to be worried? " Jack asks.

Pursing his lips, Joseph takes a moment to think his answer through. "Yes, there was. I haven't heard of him coming out of his fugue state enough to care about other packs in decades. However that being said, does not mean he's going to let the death of a son pass if indeed Falco really was his son. And that I don't know." Rocking back and forth from heel to toe gives a better clue to the degree of his worry more than his words. Jack knows when his "cowboy" slips into Josephs' speech there is cause for concern.

With a big breath and exhale Jack lets Joseph go for the evening too. "I have to speak with my father, but we'll continue this soon."

Nodding his understanding, he drawls "I'll get the handy-man over here in the next day or so to fix that."

Walking to the back of the house gives Jack a moment to change the direction his thoughts and think about what to say. How to approach his father. Placing his hand on the closed doors knob, he still pauses for a brief second to give Liam time to realize he's there. Jack opens the door without invitation but closes it softly behind him. The room still contains the king bed his mother and father have slept in for years. The pictures on the wall are all the families vacations over the years showing both him and his brother in varying stages and ages. He can still smell his mother's belongings in her dresser as well as the walk-in closet even though she's been gone a year. Her long dead cell link and pad are still sitting on top of the dresser as if just waiting for her to return.

***

I toss the rifle across my bed. Oddly I find I am not mad at Falco or his pack. I understand in some twisted way they did think we stole the girl.

Of course, once mated he should have understood that wasn't the case, but 'you can't reason with an old wolf' is a pack saying, well, for a reason. Falco was old, that much I knew. Like maybe even hundreds of years old. Maybe he'd have lived longer if he had understood about ranged weapons, I chuckle to myself. The wolf in me is satisfied with the outcome, though the rending and tearing of flesh is always satisfying as well. But as said by Thoreau 'men have become the tools of their tools' and as such, I liked mine.

"Dad, we have to talk" Coming in unbidden my youngest son says softly. Wolf ears are very good at hearing and with almost the whole pack milling about the house, Jack doesn't want to have to explain himself or seem weak. I glance at the walk-in closet and with a nod push myself off the bed. Long ago the oversized closet, more of a small room really had been made into a safe room and as such we had since discovered, was immune to wolven hearing once the door is closed.

In a more normal tone of voice Jack continues "Dad, you can't keep shooting wolves – or anyone for that matter. How am I going to defend that to the other Alphas once word gets out? And you know it will, if it hasn't already." Pausing, I think he is giving me time to explain or justify but I only look at him with a calm but subtle defiance. Shaking his head Jack continues "When you killed Danny last year his entire family packed up and moved to another pack. And while understandable, you now know I don't need to be defended in such a way. What would happen if everyone with a beef started shooting at us?" The tension in his neck gives rise to his scent being stronger, more dominant.

The top of my grey hair only comes to my youngest sons chin but that doesn't stop me from looking him in the eye. "We defend what is ours." I say softly. "This I'll defend is more than a motto, its a promise." Patrick steps into the room, hoping to dispel a fight he fears is coming, softly closing the door behind him. Jack purses his lips inhaling deeply trying to give himself time to think of a suitable non-combative response. He's always known his old man was stubborn. So had his mother been for that matter. Together his parents had often butted heads, and loudly, as humans. But this wasn't a time to butt heads. This was a time to calm down and find a new direction. One that hopefully didn't include killing any more wolves from other packs. Making his mind up in that split second Jack asks "And to that point dad, I have a job for you. One the rest of the pack can't know about."

Things Best Done In Secret

"Are you sure this a good idea?" The tall werewolf in human seeming asked. Patrick was always more reserved in his thinking and this idea or plan or whatever we choose to call it, far exceeded that.

Jack looked at his older brother and smiled. "I guess we'll find out, won't we." He had to look up at him, but only by a tiny bit. Both brothers towered over six feet tall but older brother Patrick was just about an inch taller. A fact he loved to take advantage of as all older brothers do. Yet it was Jack, brown hair with matching doe brown eyes who, as Alpha of the Phoenix Pack it was all of the included wolves who owed him deference and obedience. To an outsider, Jack had seemingly inherited this position from the former now deceased Alpha. But that's not how wolf packs work.

Mark had been killed in what had other-wise been a coordinated effort by the pack and affiliated law enforcement to bring to heel an illicit fighting ring. This involved not just the wolves but zombies who had been given a new and enhanced drug that somehow stimulated their neurons and gave them super movie quality killing skills. Notably among them was incredible speed, a partial return of dexterity and an insatiable desire to feed on anything still breathing. As if they weren't dangerous enough, this had made them exceptionally dangerous.

The cohesion of the packs round-up had fallen apart when a couple of rogue wolves who had been missed in the initial take downs. They, in a misguided attempt to get away, had released an entire group of these A-mpd zombies loose with most given the direction of a busy hotel and restaurant via an old underground service tunnel that allowed large equipment and workers easy access to and from the business and their parking all safely underground out of site. When the illegal drug spurred the released zombies on to new heights of damage and grisly murder, they did so by accessing the population through those old but clearly not unused tunnels. It was during this confusion and mass chaos that the Phoenix Pack had lost its Alpha along with several other members. Some of those members had been individuals with the bad guys and some had been a part of the good guys. Can werewolves be called good guys? Well, some days, some of us were.

Jack and Patrick had only been wolves for a short while, less than a year when this all had occurred. The Phoenix Pack had for quite some time been the most famous of the US werewolf packs. We were used to a certain level of attention and notoriety. It was not only that we were out to the public and therefore the most likely to be videoed, confronted and from time to time protested against. Thanks to Mark and his human mate Cindy, we had secured governmental contracts with cities, counties and even the state to well not kill but final end their growing zombie problem.

Myrna's had started off as the waking dead. Soon social media had nicknamed them Myrna because of the response to the M-RNA serum anti-bodies the government had mandated for several years. When a person "died" now it was no longer final. If you had received enough of those serum injections over the course of your life, you would still move about af-ter brain death. People were caught on camera watching from within their coffins, turning their heads, blinking. Then soon those people got out of their coffins and started performing daily functions such as making coffee, typing or cleaning. Whatever their muscle memory in life was strongest the newly turned Myrna's continued to perform those tasks until disturbed.

Always fun to be driving down the freeway and see some "body" driving a car. But here's the problem. As soon as there was ample interference in that muscle memory function, BOOM full on raging zombie. Although even that too became its own social media craze.

The problem was, it was disturbing the economy, or so the pundits claimed. Who knew? Entire law firms had sprung up for wrongful death for not controlling a rampaging grandpa or vehicle accident. Law suits bankrupted people, insurance companies failed to pay claims or simply dropped whole families while other companies catered to build cages for containment and zoo windows for allowing your loved ones to stay in the home. But then werewolves came on the scene.

Somehow in all of this, Mark and the Pack became the good guys. Saving or maybe just protecting humanity from itself. That contract became the basis for all werewolves to have jobs without fear of retaliation. For every "final rest" as it came to be called, the pack gained a ten percent tithe, while the remainder of the fee the werewolf team earned and split. No longer were we relegated to the shadows, hiding.

Jack, as far as anyone knew, was the youngest Alpha ever, at not quite twenty years of age. Since the incident last year, the Phoenix Pack was smaller these days admittedly. His father Liam had officially joined after their mother's death, in that same incident that had taken their Alpha. Whereas Ellan, the boys mother, had never formally joined the pack. Her boys had only been official members for a short while. It was all very convoluted to the outside world. But at its heart wolves were basic creatures. Their dominance was driven by only a few factors. Those who needed protecting and those who needed to be obeyed. Now those factors could be very very fluid but that was the gist of it.

Right now, Jack had just proposed such an idea that would break many of those tenants and quite a few contracts as well, placing the entire packs status potentially in question.

Patrick reminds them "You just told us, under no circumstances were we to go into California." He emphasizes this pointing to the front of the home, as if they all weren't aware of the meeting that had just occurred, been interrupted and then finished.

Shaking his head, Jack acknowledges "I know. But family looks after one another, even when not pack."

His voice raising a bit, "You don't even like Lillith, and no one's heard from Uncle Josh." Patrick pauses not wanting to push too hard. His concern is written all over his face. Their father, Liam hasn't spoken since the plan was proposed, but is looking thoughtful. Feeling a bit more confident since getting no immediate push back, he continues further "I know dad needs to lay low for a while. Everyone keeps mumbling about notifying the Master Alpha. Who in the hell or what in the hell even is a Master Alpha? Have you ever heard of him, this, them?" Bowing his head a bit gives Patrick the respite from challenging his Alpha outright.

"I have to admit, I have not," Jack responds "But that doesn't mean it's not something we haven't encountered before. In the world of wolf, we are babies in diapers." Liam smirks at that. "Look, I think this will kill two birds with one stone. Dad gets to "disappear" for a while and hopefully he can safely escort our aunt-by-marriage and niece and nephew here to safety. We know they are on their way. They are coming whether we like it or not."

Liam quietly inserts "We made a promise, your mother and I, to Joshua."

"I know dad, and I am good with that. Of course they can come here. I'm just saying, right now might not be the best time to go and meet them. Let them find their own way here." Even as Patrick finishes the sentence he can tell he's overstepped. His dad's scent flushes in annoyance and involuntarily a lip half curls even in human form. A gentle knock on the closets room door thankfully distracts the three men from rising tensions. Even as established as they are in order and succession, being in such close quarters when not aligned in their thoughts and intentions could readily allow for an explosion of dominance. It would seem Patrick's recent mating has emboldened him to the point of insubordination.

Without invitation, Bethy steps into the room. Rarely in her human form, the tiny woman is in every way as breathtaking as her wolf. Long flowing red hair, emerald green eyes, tiny slip of a waist and standing a mere five foot three. She looks the antithesis of the room's other current inhabitants. In her hand she is carrying a pair of silvered material items.

"What about these?" she asks, keeping her eyes averted. Individually she doesn't fear any of the men in the room but being the lowest of the wolves in the pack, even her human form can't help but feel nervous. She holds her hand out to Liam. The shiny silver material being offered in it. Liam takes them and examines them. Stretching them out, twisting them back and forth.

Looking up at Jack he asks "What are these?"

Taking them from his father, he gives a sigh. "Well, not really ready for the world yet. A developer came to me asking if we'd be the test pack for these. They are basically a neck wrap for a wolf. This guy, Derrick saw videos of the many wolves fighting the Myrna's last year and thought how vulnerable we were to their bites. It only takes one good bite and we are done for. So he was already working on a super light Kevlar with new nanofibers and infused them with these commercially available cooling neck wraps. The Crows nest was brought in on it, and we have a few to test out. He wanted to do a whole body suit kind of thing, but I said most wolves wouldn't go for anything that constricting and he came back with these." Turning to look at the spritely girl "I just got these Bethy, how did you know about them?"

Shyly "Who do you think gets the mail around here?"

Patrick snickers, "She's got ya there little bro." And just like that tensions ratchet down to a less confrontational level and the room seems to expand.

Nicking them back quicker than either boy would have given him credit for, Liam says "Well there's no time like the present." And pulls one of them over his head to rest around his neck loosely.

"Look, just make sure they make it safely out dad. Lillith is not exactly well, built for this" Jack says with snorts all around. "The point is you can change either direction with it still on."

"Well if you boys, and madam, will get out of my bedroom closet I will shift into my wolf and we can go see if I can save your aunt and her kids."

It's the next morning before they hear from Lillith's daughter Shiela. They exchange information, find out the family made it out safely and are on the road into Arizona. Having more access to up to the minute news they help navigate the many closures and places being reported as overrun from the zombies. The quake has seemed to awaken them all down the fault line. Even the ones in their own state have taken an up-tick in activity and more werewolf teams have had to be deployed. Pack mates Jim along with his working partner Dale had departed for Reno while a submissive mated pair of wolves Andy and Amy had agreed to travel to Las Vegas to help out there. They claimed to want to pay their house off early and had no kids, so making their choice seem more reasonable.

The brothers Ramon and Isaac had been forced to stay though they too had volunteered. With Isaac still being in high school however no one thought this was a good plan. It did cause a momentary ruffle of fur, but the boys had been given the task of patrolling the house after classes to ensure no stray Festival Pack decided to try to take retribution. It kept them occupied and staying at the house which suited them.

Joshua, the Fallen

Falling. I remember this huge pressure of sound as if someone had boxed both my ears from behind and then falling. Falling falling falling I might have yelped. Then the world went black.

I have no idea how long I was out. But coming to, proved to be a bit of a challenge. My eyes slowly opened, albeit independently and a bit fuzzy. I tried closing them again and willing them to work together. After a few more false starts, they seemed to cooperate a little bit better. I find I can turn my head, so I do. Looking around me knocks the loose dust from my face to trickle onto the cement patch I am laying on. Taking stock of my body, I realize while I don't think anything is broken my head is swimming with each turn that I don't think is entirely due to my eyes continuing lack of focus. I stir my limbs in an attempt to get up.

My mind flashes back to before the falling and my eyes widen. "Dan!" I yell. In reality my yell comes out as just a croak but at least I am making sound. My chest hurts with the effort. Licking dust coated lips, I try again. "Dan!" To my left there is a soft growl from one very big dog. Startled, I try to turn my body towards the animal and see that between us, is my partners partially obscured body with two rather thick pieces of rebar sticking obscenely out from it. One pierces his torso, the other a leg. It's clear Dan has been dead for several hours I judge since his blood no longer runs freely. "Aw Dan, what am I going to tell your wife?" I think. He'd only been with the force four years in total and the last two as my partner. Dan is, or rather was, I correct myself mentally; a really decent fellow and not everyone who does our job can that be said about.

Given that reminder, I look around for the suspect we had handcuffed just a few minutes prior to the collapse of this building this is all around us. A young-ish man we had secured in handcuffs while we ran his identicard. Caught him stealing a car and hadn't been able to confirm his identity at the time.

Glancing around I don't find another body evident but the large dog comes nearer and clearer into focus. Browns and greys with some black on the tip of his nose. He lifts a single lip at me. I'm not too sure but I think this is a werewolf and may in fact be the arrested suspect. My sister Ellan and her husband are werewolves and they say however much you weigh as a human is how much you weigh as a wolf. My befuddled mind says this looks to be right.

I try sitting up and find this manageable but it begins a maelstrom of a headache and some lovely stomach gut-wrenching nausea. "Scott?" I ask in a croaky voice. The canine in question sneezes once at me then opens his mouth and begins panting. I have no idea if that's an affirmative or not. "Okay, so I have zero evidence, thoughts, no wait give me a minute," I stutter out. Trying again, "You're Scott, yes?" The dog nods his head slowly up and down. "Okay good. I'm Officer, no sorry Josh. My name is Josh Cawley." I find my throat getting dryer by the moment and I begin to cough. Scott the werewolf looks at me and softly whines then begins looking around us, for what I'm not sure.

Just then my partner stirs, opening and closing his mouth. Oh God, I think. Quickly hitting the emergency button on my radio while trying to key my microphone I yell "Officer down, Officer down!". The werewolf advances to my partner grabbing him by the throat and ripping it out so quickly my brain can't quite catch up. The head lolls to one side remaining only attached by a few pieces of meat and gristle. Instinctively I fumble for my gun but my limbs are still not quite responding to my demands just yet. My gun is not in its holster.

This evil creature just killed my partner, my brain screams. But another, different sound distracts me and I turn my head to slowly focus on two of what I guess could only be called people, crawling out of the dark and into our space of collapsed car parking. One is just pulling his upper torso along with no matching lower torso snapping his jaws at us as if from some B rated movie my wife seems to love. The other drags herself along the floor while part of her lower legs are missing. Horrified to see sticks of bone looking like a child's plaything following behind her in some bizarre dead come to life thing. I am frozen in place and am unable to move. I can only gape in terror. Scott, the werewolf gets up and paces over to the closest one who is the half man. He repeats his throat ripping doing to him exactly as he has just done to my partner only this time further ripping the man's head from his shoulders. The head rolls to the side for a moment before completely falling off and thudding to the ground. That was not a sound I ever needed to hear. Moving on to the woman who is only recognizable as a such by her exposed breasts from the ripped material of her shirt and certainly not by her melted fleshy face, he places a large paw between her shoulders pinning her down and proceeds to rip her head from the remaining portion of her body as well. She falls to the ground covering her exposed chest, ceasing all forward movement as well. Scott takes one of his paws and tries clearing his mouth of the black goo their blood turns too, then wretches onto the remains.

I realize now what the wolf has done is stopped the Myrna's from feeding on me and him. I remember from training that noise draws them in. I hold my finger to my mouth in the universal gesture of quiet and the wolf nods. We have to go. I have a family to get back to and right now something as stupidly insignificant as a car theft isn't even on my radar.

"Scott, we've got to go." I whisper. "Do you know a way out of here?"

The wolf looks over his shoulder. Glancing, I can barely make out a tunnel. Did we really fall all three stories and into the sewer line? And how long have I been down here? There's still no response on the radio and though I've pressed the red emergency button there's also no comforting acknowledgement from there either. I can only hope my body cam is still recording.

After a couple of false starts on my part, together we work our way up some rubble, being careful to not dislodge any more than we have to. My work boots are a good fit for this kind of climb and I presume Scott isn't having too difficult of a time of it on his four paws. I have no idea why he stayed with Dan and I. Surely being wolf, it would have been easier for him to just skedaddle out of here, find someplace safe. I am desperately thirsty at this point and panting almost as much as Scott is. Together we make it up a level to daylight. The stairs are only partially collapsed and we've been able to navigate them fairly well.

It's eerie and quiet. There are no cars, no horns, no talking. In fact, no people. I reach for my cell phone only to find it snapped into more than a few pieces. My wife and kids must think, what? That I died most likely. I wonder again how long it's been. A tickle at my ear has me swiping away fresh blood. The wolf glances back at me but keeps going. They should have gotten out of the city by now and heading for my sisters in Arizona.

Ellan died last year, but her husband and their kids still live there. We had a bug out plan in place ever since my children were born. I wouldn't say I am paranoid but after what happened today can't say I am not either. Protection and safety with Ellan and Liam, both of whom were werewolves sounds pretty good right now. Both of whom are retired law enforcement. Closing my eyes tightly I can see my beautiful wife. She was never a prepper but I taught my kids things. Things I thought they should know and could handle for their ages. I have to get home. I have to make sure they got out.

A cold nose brushes my hand and without thought I drop to my knee and hug the wolf. I couldn't tell how long we stayed like this. It's embarrassing to think how I can take comfort from this total stranger, this thief. As if on cue we break apart and step out into the light of the street cautiously. I can see a few of the Myrna zombie things, still on their feet and looking more human than the ones below had. Neither of us make a sound as we slowly work our way down the street. My patrol car is nowhere to be seen. Funnily enough my brain thinks, I hope the department doesn't charge me for that. I need to find some water, and soon. Looking down at Scott I whisper "Can you take me home?" I rattle off my address. We are on the other side of town in the second most densely populated city in the US. Even though only forty-seven miles in size, the damage done from what I can now see was an earthquake has taken its toll. Roads torn apart, water spewing from underground, hissing from pipes I presume to be gas and so many milling Myrnas that I can't see a single normal human. No cars move through the streets though that would be difficult from all the debris.

I try the closest small vehicle and find it's not charged. "Damn electric cars," I curse wishing for my old Jeep Tracker at home. But if Lillith did what she was supposed to, her and the kids would safely be in Arizona by now. Ellan's family pack would protect them. She had promised me as my big sister.

I love my family dearly of course and my sister and her family, but sadly they had never gotten along. Lilith was always a bit of a trophy wife. I chuckle at the thought. And Ellan, well Ellan walked her own path. Sighing, I keep following the wolf somehow trusting him to get me where I need to go.

Turning a corner, we almost run headlong into a huge grouping of these undead. Until spotting us, they might have just been milling around waiting for their coffee for all I knew, but once we turned the corner Scott stopped dead in his tracks, clearly startled, while I turned right into him almost tripping over him and letting out a small gasp of surprise, pain and a long mumbled string of curses. Looking around for cover I find very little to protect us with. I can only think to draw out my collapsed baton, whipping it into full size and stand ready. The wolf races across the street, passing a few of the closer zombies knocking them to the ground with his shoulder. Diving cat like into the streets open storm drain he disappears into what I presume is safety. Instinct has me following suit but i am much slower from the pain and at the last minute, my utility belt prevents me from successfully sliding in. In a panic I take my pants loose and shimmy the rest of the way, narrowly avoiding grabbing hands and stumbling feet.

Falling once again, I land heavily on my side. My world swims before my eyes, threatening to black out again. Barely able to breath, I pant from both pain and the adrenaline rush of fear. Somehow, I manage to whisper, "Good spotting Scott." I clear my throat spitting out a bit of dust and bright red blood.

The depth of the fall was right around four feet so I can easily look out and see all the agitated zombies looking around for the prey that has eluded them. That prey having been Scott and I; I am quite relieved at their failure. I see my baton laying a few feet from the opening we've just squeezed through. I must have dropped it in my frenzy to get to safety. "Damn." I think. Remembering finally from my training that zombies are attracted to not just sound but movement as well, I back away a bit from the opening. Looking down at Scott, the world swims once again before my eyes and I am forced to sit on the cold cement before I fall again into the black.

Blinking rapidly, gasping for breath I come to. I must have drifted off or worse passed out because the light is no longer streaming in from above, but rather it's a small sliver in the far corner. The wolf is shaking himself spraying me with water, which I am guessing is what awakened me. In my lap, I notice a large bottle of fresh water. He must have scavenged off for it while I rested. This has been a hard day. My uniform is sticky from dried blood, building dust and road grime. I can smell myself and wish for home and a hot shower.

I don't know how long I was out this time but taking in my surroundings is more to keep my mind occupied. I see we are sitting on a large concrete ledge that leads to a deeper four- or five-foot drop into the connecting storm drain. All of these lead to the ocean if we were to follow the downward slant, but that's not my goal. I need to make it home. To make sure my family got out alright or to save them if they didn't. The wolf leans into me keeping me from tumbling over the edge so I take his advice and sit back. I'm still panting I guess from the fall, it's hard to catch my breath.

Really looking at the wolf for the first time I see things I missed before. Like how Scott has tears in his fur that look like scrapes and gouges. He too is dirty and sticky from dried blood and debris. What I mistook for a black color on his muzzle looks more to be dried blood and some road tar. And though we are not currently moving, he is holding one of his legs up, in a not quite touching the ground painful way. Guess the fall wasn't easy on him either.

I finish the proffered bottle of water and rest my head back again. I don't think I blacked out this time but when I open my eyes next it is completely dark out. Scott is laying asleep next to me, his large shaggy body although still a bit damp, comfortingly warm in the cold night air. Without thinking about it, I go to pet him as I would any canine but he whips around snarling, his jaws snapping precariously close to my face. Frozen in place I don't know what to. I can think of no way to defend myself from a seated position with no billy club, no firearm and barely able to see.

The moment passes and he backs up a step turning his head away from mine, lowering his muzzle. "It's okay," I say. "Sorry, didn't mean to treat you like a pet."

We both get up at that and stretch a bit. I've been sitting on my tailbone for so long, it is immensely painful and I am very stiff. Scott leaps down gracefully into the bottom of the drain pipe that additional four or five feet down and looks up at me. I realize he is asking me to follow. Buckling my pants and duty belt, I slide myself down the shelf and gingerly land in the boot deep water. We press on into the night my only guide his furry behind just a hairs breath ahead of me. I have no idea where we are going. I can only hope the werewolf does. With every couple of twists and turns I have to stop and lean on the cold cement wall to catch my breath. And even though I am cold, I am sweating from the exertion.

San Francisco is not a very big place. Folks often used to call it the seven by seven because it's only about forty-nine miles square. I know my home was only roughly four miles south -southeast of where we started, but in this maze of tunnels I have no idea where I am any longer. On any normal day my usual workout routine almost always includes several miles on the incline treadmill. But right now, there is a burning in my chest and my vision is still blurry so I follow, almost meekly, behind the wolf, trusting him to know the way and keep me safe.

Stopping now. means we are standing in almost six inches of rainwater. I guess I should be thankful it's just water and we didn't end up in a sewer line. Every time we pass an entry point to the street, I just look at the rebar ladder and question if I have the strength to lift the manhole cover. Since my phone became a jig saw puzzle, I have no idea how much time has passed but we keep going.

Finally, after what seems like a tortured eternity, the wolf stops his trek and points his nose to one particular manhole cover. Placing both hands on my knees bending over almost double I pant out "Give me a sec."

The tiniest shaft of light creeps through a crack in the metal ring holding the cover in place. We traveled longer than I thought. Resolving myself to the pain, I climb most of the way up the metal ladder stopping a few rungs short of the top. Now that I'm here, I'm not sure how to open this, short of brute force,which right now is not my strong suit. While looking up at the cover debating with myself, I feel the wolf run up my back and slam his shoulder into the cover, popping it up and loose. Not being a cat, he falls to the ground heavily with a splash. I'm frozen to the rungs watching this play out before dropping myself to check on my fallen... what are we exactly? Comrades? Friends? Frenemies? I have no words for this, but lower myself to the ground to check on Scott. The wolf is slowly getting up but holding his head to the side a bit. Damn, I hope he didn't hurt himself; I have no medical skills beyond the basic CPR we are required to be proficient in. I run my hands down him feeling for what I'm not sure but somehow it settles us both. He gives a small whine while indicating the now slightly ajar cover letting in a marginally larger shaft of mornings glow.

I climb back up to the top and look out onto the small sliver of street visible. I can see many moving bodies, all of them the dead. Just how many of these things are there, I think? My brain grinds into gear and I remember that several of the islands and abandoned warehouses were used to house the dead rather than destroy them, believing it to be a curable condition rather than some bizarre death. Gotta love a humanistic approach, but not so much right now.

Glancing around I recognize several visible landmarks. This is my street. My heart leaps with joy. I want to run out there, to my home. But being my street doesn't mean being close enough to see my home. And from what I can see, the entire south side of the street has collapsed in on itself sinking several feet. The ground slopes normally but this angle is very extreme. It might only be half a block to what should be my home, but what if it's not even there?

Closing my eyes a moment I tell myself not to think that way. That Lillith and the children are fine. A water geyser on the far side, sprays high into the air and the electricity would seem to be off because the many downed power lines remain still and silent. Turning to face Scott I ask "If I can lift this cover high enough can you jump free? We'll have to make a run for it once topside. I'm sure those undead will zero in on us in seconds. If we can make it to my house, and it's still standing, we should be able to blockade at least the garage. I've reinforced that door." The only response I get is a slow whine. I'm still not sure we are communicating here. Leaning down in order to keep my voice low I say "Let me raise the cover with my shoulders as far as I can and you do that jump climb thing again and make a beeline for the house. I'll be right behind you." The wolf tips his head at me narrowing his eyes. Okay so much for that idea, I think.

Taking a look around I don't see any immediate street level drain openings. I don't remember if there is one closer to my home or not. It's risky but I climb back up to the top peering out again. Looking down at Scott, I implore him again "Please, my home is literally four houses down, I just can't see it. You got us this far. Just a little bit further." Without waiting for a response, I raise myself bracing my shoulder and back on the cover and push with my legs. This raises me up far enough I think I can actually wriggle my way out of here if this ringing in my ears would just give me a moments peace. Pushing myself further, I am able to get most of my torso out of the drain. It's then I realize how many of the in-a-zombie state Myrna's there really are. The whole area is littered with them. Gasping for breath since the manhole cover is laying across my lower spine, I continue to wriggle but this time, being more careful to make less noise. Scott doesn't seem to want to be left behind as he climbs up the iron rungs and sticks his head out glancing around as well. He has no perch to be able to lift himself off and I twist, grabbing him by the scruff of the neck like some naughty cat and drag him up into the daylight. He scrambles ungraciously onto the streets blacktop and whines softly pointing his nose at a few of the closest zombies who have started to take notice of us. In their mindless shambling, they have turned and seem to be deciding if we are making enough noise to be interesting or not. I freeze in place trying not to gasp for breath with this heavy weight still across me. Thankfully Scott understands the assignment and remains still as well. I can't judge time, but after a while the dead go back to shuffling along the street, in search of what I do not care to know.

I begin an inchworm-like wriggle drawing my body further out from the drain until it's just my feet left trapped by the weight. My ankles are too weak by themselves to release my feet; I am too exhausted to roll over and remove myself and my adrenaline crashed a long time ago. Scott nudges his nose underneath giving me a bit of release and I slide my feet free when I point my toes. That is not something easily done when wearing heavy leather steel-toed boots with a two-inch-thick sole on them.

Scott's puffing his cheeks out just to breath due to the pressure on his poor muzzle. Feeling around on my duty belt I can only come up with my taser for anything of substance to be able to wedge underneath the cover to release Scott as well as keep it from slamming down and drawing attention to ourselves.

Released from his self-imposed trap, we make our way slowly towards my home. I try mimicking the shambling movements of the dead, keeping my head low but my eyes scanning for any sudden interest. We seem to be succeeding. I have a clear eye line to my home and mercifully it's still standing. My heart races, then pounds. Getting closer, I can see the garage door is open. I almost cry out with relief. They must have made it out. Lillith, Jason and Sheila all must have made it out. I'm not focusing as well as I could in my haste to make sure my family made it out safely.

A sound to my side calls my attention away and I see Scott knocking down one of the dead who has gotten disparagingly close. I stomp on its neck again and again until there is nothing but a puddle of black tar like goo with tinges of red in it. Glancing around I can tell we have now become the focus of several of the closer zombies. Mrs. Gliven stumbles her way towards us mouth agape but chewing, hands clutching. I didn't particularly like her or her little poodle dog that pooped on my step every morning but I didn't wish this on her either. A large gash in her head has torn away most of her hair and an eye but somehow that doesn't stop her from coming for Scott and I. Others are following her lead, drawn to her change in direction maybe. There's no point in pretending any further, the wolf and I run for the open garage slamming it shut behind us. I had it reinforced a few years ago when some civil unrest caused me concern so hearing it's snap and click gives me reassurance enough to fall to my knees and gasp for breath. I am finding it increasingly difficult to draw deep breaths and running has not helped. I collapse a bit further with my hands flat on the cement trying desperately to draw breath. Scott tugs a small single mattress over to me and I fully collapse onto it. The rumpled sheets I recognize as my sons from his latest phase of super hero worship.

Blinking slowly, I try to get up but find my body won't respond. I am lying on my back, still on my son's mattress in our lower-level garage. Once again, Scott's warm furry werewolf body is pressed up against mine keeping me warm. He stirs when I do, stretching like a giant sleepy house pet. He looks down at me giving a soft whine. My vision is cloudy and dark. Realization hits me. I am dying. I am home but I am dying. It's now been three days by my reckoning since the earthquake event and whatever damage was done in the initial fall has almost finished its work of killing me. Another realization hits me as well. Once dead, I will become like all those other Myrnas out there. The shambling dead zombies. I wish I could see my family one last time. Tell them I love them. Kiss my wife, hug my kids. But I got so much more than so many. I at least got to go home.

Fumbling slowly in my breast pocket I pull out a small spiral notebook. It's a little three by five in shape, army green with water resistant paper so officers can make notes in the moist San Francisco climate. The mini pen with it is still strung through its rungs. Flipping it open to an empty page I begin to write a note to my family. How much I love them, how proud I am. How much I miss them and will miss my children growing up. All the things I wanted to say to my wife over the years. It's a long list.

Liliths Run To Safety

By the end of the first day's travel, we've reached the stopping point Joshua indicated on the map according to Sheila. I am so tired. Exhausted really. According to the notes he left us for driving from San Francisco, leaving our home and going to Los Angeles, it should have taken five and one-half hours. With road closures, detours, road debris, broken lanes, stopped or abandoned vehicles and the milling Myrna zombie people, it's taken me closer to nine. My nerves are shot. I am shaking as if I've overdosed on caffeine. And there had been bodies. So many bodies. Fresh ones in pieces with limbs missing and some areas slick with their bright red or darkening ruby bodily fluids. I saw the zombies, as I now know they really are, eating the red flesh and pulling great strands of what could only be intestines up to their putrid mouths. I feel like a worn to a frazzle movie extra in some horror flick. Only this doesn't seem to end. I keep waiting for a director to call cut but it doesn't happen.

Jason has kept himself busily charging all of our devices while playing games the whole way, allowing the vehicle to charge all of our electronics. I don't think he even looked up once or noticed. Sheila, who is still seated in the passenger's side next to me, remained wide eyed and silent, other than for the occasional directions, watching the whole way. Seeing everything the same as me.

We finally had cell reception when we hit Fresno and were able to get some gas. The price's had tripled overnight of course, but we were able to fill up. Credit card usage was spotty and sometimes outright refused. Joshua, it turns out, had kept a stash of cash in his bug out bag, run bag... I'm not sure what he called it. Gratefully we used the restrooms here, changed clothes, washed our faces and continued on. But that was the last of the courtesy restrooms.

I had had to stop to nap in a pretty little rest stop nestled between some rolling hills outside all of the major city areas. There are many others doing the same thing. Everyone is staying shut into their cars. No one speaks to anyone beyond the head nod or curt hello. I see some of the other women crying. What I wouldn't give for a good cry right now. A few drivers have injured passengers. Some of the cars bear the marks of gore on them, indicating they too had to drive through what were once people. I can only imagine what our vehicle looks like. During one rest stop we had to leave in haste because a large group of shambling zombies had come wandering through and began banging on any window where people or animals were visible. I'm so scared. I just want to breakdown. A lot of the highway exits have been closed and are being guarded. Cities don't want us. They have even gone so far as to barricade some of the exits in a few places.

The kids and I spend a few hours sleeping at yet another rest area only to be rousted out of there by officials attempting to once again, close off access. Trying to exit to find fuel is an ordeal. We can't just stop at the closest station. There are too many homeless. Too many zombies. Too many vagabonds who will rob us or worse. I'm not sure who I fear more, the human thieves or the dead. Each time we have to pull over, my beautiful daughter who just days ago was worried about her history exam, brings the gun onto her lap, covering it with her jacket. She keeps the muzzle pointed towards whatever group of people are closest and has this look on her face I can't even describe. Fear, determination, anxiety. I think even Jason is beginning to feel the effects of it. He sits hunched down in his seat. He's taken to covering everything with the silver space blankets so no one can easily see that we carry supplies. Twice he's gone through his dad's bag counting everything as if taking inventory. Maybe he is.

By day two, I am thinking I understand how the zombies feel. Time slows and the day crawls by with us following this same routine. I didn't know I could be this exhausted. I don't normally drive, let alone this marathon. I didn't realize there were so many desolate areas coming nearer and nearer to the Arizona border. Food isn't a problem thank goodness. Sheila had filled two reusable grocery bags with edible goodies which became a life saver in more ways than I can count. Stored in the back and handed out by Jason, we've had boxes of cereal, crackers, cookies, cheese and even some juice boxes along with the fruit from the counter. When did my children get so resourceful?

The further we travel I thought for sure, some sense of normalcy would return. But that's not the case. Initially there were no cars on the roads but as we hit the combined Angles area it became a nightmare. People were forcefully taken from their vehicles. Sometimes by zombies, sometimes by roving bands of thugs. The further we traveled east out of Angles the cars were thinning out on the roads. But that led to more abandoned vehicles for lack of gas and more bodies. I don't know what killed them. And I don't give it too close a look. Radio reception remained overall very good, however once out of the immediate area the news was no longer filled with the dead, families lost and damage done by the quake. It was if the rest of the world didn't want to acknowledge what had transpired. Even when it was being reported that some towns had gone so far as to isolate themselves, not allowing travelers or non-residents to enter these were only brief mentions. Many mountain towns had isolated themselves with local broadcasting giving us open or closed exit points.

One thing that is being announced ad nauseam over the radio was that Arizona, our final destination, has closed its borders to only their own residents. I have no idea what we are going to do once we reach that check point. Joshua wanted us to go to his sister's, saying they could protect us, and we have been able to make a few calls to our Arizona relatives But how do I get my kids and myself through a checkpoint? We don't live there. Jack keeps telling us everything will be okay and to just get to the meeting point. But he's just a kid himself. He was only eighteen when his mom died and he took over as, what do they call it pack leader or something? Ugh, I can't believe I am deliberately driving into a dog pack. No one seems to be able to get Liam on the phone. Why isn't he leading them? He's their father. I just want to go home to my pretty bi-level and back to my normal life.

We start seeing more of the Myrna zombie things once again as we approach more civilized areas. Even stopping at the now guarded rest stops is so frightening to me. Men with guns are everywhere, some in uniforms, and more ominously some not. People in large RV's are being robbed for what others perceive as having supplies, but more frequently they just run out of gas and have to abandon them by the roadside. I learned from Sheila to stay away from them. When did she get to be so smart? We hide all of our packs at our feet or underneath the pillows and blankets Jason brought. At night we have to cover the windows so we don't draw attention to ourselves.

By day four Sheila's regular calls to Ellan's house in Arizona get picked up due to cell service being restored but this only leaves me more worried. Her son's Patrick and Jack are there. They've answered all of our calls but then they say their father is still in his wolf form and can't come to the phone yet. What does that mean? What am I walking into? What am I taking my children into? This can't possibly be better than getting a motel and just waiting for Joshua to find us. I just want my husband to find us. Tears regularly stream down my face. Why hasn't he called? How could I have thought this was a good idea? Leaving our home, the kids' school, and friends. It was just an earthquake, right? We've had earthquakes before. Every stop is an opportunity for me to call Joshua's cell. Always with no response. If i could just here his voice, know he's okay.

"MOM!" Sheila screams while bracing her hands on the dash. Coming back to the moment, I see the highway is blocked with a large what I can only call herd of these zombie things all milling about. In creepy unison they halt their meandering shuffle and turn facing my vehicle because I have slammed on the brakes hard enough to cause my vehicle to turn into a skid. We have gained their unwanted attention.

Sitting sideways on the road with this overwhelming hoard now stumbling, tripping and lumbering towards us I can only think Oh my God. We've came so close to making it into Arizona. What do we do now? My vision swims and blackness threatens to overtake me. I am having a hard time breathing, my chest hurts to match my headache, but I have to get us out of here somehow. The first of the hoard reaches the side of the car. It's the side my kids are on. I'm frozen yet I can hear myself scream. Jason is crying from the back seat, yelling something at me. Sheila has grabbed my arm which is still clutching the steering wheel while yelling "MOM, MOM we have to GO!"

The car bucks from side-to-side rocking back and forth. Adding to my terror, a huge dog leaps from nowhere, onto the hood. He is so large he covers the entire hood of my vehicle only keeping himself from sliding down the front into the mass of the dead with his enormous claws embedded into the metal, flicking paint chips into the air. His light brown coat is shaggy and there's a splash of white across his face looking like an old healed scar. He has a silver bandanna on and my brain stops to take in the absurdity of that.

He stares into the windshield, at me. Just stares at me for what must only be a fraction of a second, but in that moment, I know I have failed. He has told me with his look, I have failed. I have killed whomever that wolf is. And possibly my children as well. Snorting or maybe sneezing once, the wolf digs his nails into my paint and launches himself into the mass of dead things now pounding on the sides of my vehicle.

To my horror I watch him as he uses his extraordinary size to bowl through the mass of what was once humanity. Most are so focused on landing blows on my vehicle they don't seem to notice him initially and dozens fall down to the ground, losing their footing under his immense bulk. It's then I realize he isn't killing them, only knocking them over, creating a kind of path. Sheila resumes her scream of "Go!" and this time I don't need to be told twice.

I turn the car into the path the wolf seems to be creating, driving over the downed bodies. If I think for even a second they are people, I will be sick.

He had taken them by surprise at first, but now their attention has turned to him and they are single-mindedly focused on tearing him to pieces. I can't see him any longer and the path is now more a trickle.

I push the accelerator down thinking I have lost him. But as I speed up it's clear he is being overwhelmed by these things. Honking my horn, I hope maybe to draw their attention. I see blood on his large furred shoulder and it seems to be dripping from other places as well. Is it his? Is he hurt? Flaps of skin seem to be missing as if pulled away. My honking has drawn some of the remaining hoard's attention, which does indeed seem to be thinning out. Subconsciously I notice Jason has stopped yelling and is more whimpering. I don't know when I stopped shrieking but at some point, I to have stopped as well.

Panting as if I just had a hard run at the gym, I watch the large wolf falter and loose his footing. He looks done in. His breath coming in ragged gasps. His blood runs in bright red rivulets down a shoulder wound and from other smaller injuries. I slow again so as not to run over him, but that allows more of the dead to close the circle.

It takes only a fraction of a second and we are encircled again. Having to stop with the wolf right under my front bumper, I can't move unless I run him over. A second clattering of nails on the top of my stopped SUV has all of us jumping. So intent were we on the scene out our front windshield the new wolf on top of us gave us an even bigger start. This wolf slides down the front windshield then also leaps from the top of my hood into the fray. I'm not even sure this is a wolf, she looks to be no more than a large dog. The fur is a golden red, but also with the funny silvered bandanna. It disappears, not into the gathering of dead but rather underneath my vehicle. I can't see it or the first wolf any longer. What am I supposed to do now?

Shots ring out. I know that sound. Gunfire. Several more of the undead group drop. Someone is out there. Someone human, who can help us. I step on the accelerator forgetting there could be a werewolf underneath my tires. My only thought is to get myself and my kids out of here safely.

The road clears as I break free leaving the mass of bodies behind. Approaching the hill indicating the check point outside of the borders small city and leading into Arizona and what I can only pray to be is safety on the other side. That must be where the shots came from. I can see the fencing, the cars and the people. Actual people. We can do this, I think. I speed up, now with a clear goal in mind. The first outer security gate slides open while some uniformed men sit in towers and shoot at more of the moving dead. The silver chain link gait slides closed behind us. It's over, we are safe. I begin shaking, more tears streaming down my face. Taking in great gulping gasps of air. I stop the car, even managing to turn it off, but can't seem to let go of the steering wheel.

The uniformed soldier knocks on my window indicating for me to roll it down.

Liam's Rescue At The Families Arrival

From Sheila and Jason's calls we know they are close. The border won't let them pass without some kind of evidence they have residence in Arizona. Jack has collaborated with Cindy, who still handles all of the Phoenix Packs finances and contracts, to get something outlined and legal. I have spent the greater part of this time scouting ahead and seeing which is the best crossing point without getting caught. As wolf I could swim across the Colorado river. This time of year it's not very swift or deep but I tire easily and I fear it will take a greater toll on me than I am prepared for.

Earlier in the day I had made the short drive from Phoenix to the California border. With the crossing effectively closed there wasn't much traffic going this direction and I made excellent time. Changing to my wolf self is always slow and painful and today was no exception, but I had come prepared. A large laundry style tub of fresh water in the back of the van sitting next to an old fashioned cooler filled with meats, the lid tucked behind it for both safety and so I can find it later. I suspect I'll be too weak to change for a while and will have to rely on these supplies until I can muster the strength. One of the pack members has a friend who lives out here, so thankfully I was able to park the car safely in their side yard. Less chance of thieves coming along and destroying to taking it or my supplies.

All I have to do is protect them from the horde of milling zombies, I say all. That's a tall order. Maybe they won't even need my help and they'll be smart enough to contact the check point ahead of time. Driving through them shouldn't be all that difficult if they just keep going without any deviations or sudden moves. The border patrol agents have been laying down suppressive fire in the form of flame throwers to those trying to make it to the crossover point. Effectively creating a wall of fire on both sides for a vehicle to drive down.

Watching as another car creeps its way to the checkpoints ten foot tall chain link fence I notice things. Like move slow enough the herd doesn't pay you any attention. This car had its windows all blacked out so there was no motion to be seen – only the windshield remained clear. The car crept through the mass of zombies excruciatingly slow. The final quarter of a mile or so must have taken them over twenty minutes, but it worked. Zombies barely noticed and really just bounced off the car softly when nudged from its movement. The first gate slides open admitting the car sliding closed behind it only admitting one stray zombie who somehow seemed to be hooked on the passengers side mirror and dragged along for the ride. The soldiers made quick work of the unwanted hitchhiker and processed the family inside in a quick and efficient manner. Arizona plates, and I could tell Arizona ID's. Even taking the time to run a full vein pattern biometrics took I would guess less than three minutes. The family inside the car was waved through the second set of chain link gates and off they sped. Interesting, usually they have a nurse check everyone out, insuring no bite wounds or other injuries.

In my werewolf form, they shouldn't question me too closely. Wolves who get bitten and saliva or zombie blood into their bodies turn almost instantly into ravening creatures whose only release comes from a bullet to the head. Absentmindedly I rub the silver enhanced Kevlar bandana between my throat and the fence. I'd been watching the check point for several hours, different cars coming through, all creeping painfully slow. The same procedure every time. Creep, creep, gates open, enter and close. ID's checked and off they go. I wonder what happens if someone tries to enter and is not an Arizona resident? I am sure hoping Cindy and Jack have the information updated or entered or whatever it is they needed to do. How are Lillith and the kids going to gain entry? The hours roll on and I find myself dozing off. Better find a closer spot. One on their side of the fence.

Wandering around a bit, the Colorado river is nice and cool on my paws but I do know it can deepen and the current run swift. I'm not as strong a swimmer as I once was. Needing to stay hidden and not let the guards see me, I head for Gilligan's Island but see it has somehow become the new destination spot for the red-necks of Arizona to spot, sight and shoot zombies from. All safely situated near the middle of the Colorado river on the Arizona side. Okay need a new plan here folks, I think, and quickly. It's rapidly approaching the time Sheila said they should be reaching the boarder. Trotting back towards the check point I find a spot of sand that seems softer and dig my way under the fence line. Frowning, I turn and rub my shoulder across the chain link pulling out bits of fur so I can find my way back should it be necessary or others from the pack can know where I crossed. Communication is always important.

The heat is starting to bother me already and I begin to pant. There's not much cover over here as I make my way, following the fence line back towards the check point. I'll have to cross the bridge in full view of not only the soldiers but the zombies in order to make it further into the restricted zone. Closer to where my wife's family is soon to be. No one's heard from Joshua since this all happened. As law enforcement you expect to be in the thick of things, but I fear the worst has happened. A couple of alert soldiers point me out as I pad my way across the open space. The silver Kevlar is hotter than I anticipated, I sure hope it works. A burned out car serves as a shady resting spot, one I can fully hide my shaggy body from the milling herd of undead.

Coming closer in the distance an ugly green off road boxy vehicle speeds into sight. She's going too fast, who ever that is. A mantra starts in my head slow down slow down slow down. Suddenly the vehicle hits its brakes, careens to the side in a loud screeching skid and comes to a halt. Every zombie within a mile heard that and most saw it. It unison like some creepy army all pulled by the same lever the zombies turn and begin encircling the stopped SUV. Damn that idiot I swear. I know Lillith doesn't drive much but is it too hard to follow simple instructions?

Leaving the shade and safety of my hiding spot I race to the vehicle. Leaping on top of it isn't terribly difficult but if there hadn't been a roof rack, I'd have slid right off and over the other side. I do manage to catch myself and instead slide down the front windshield to the hood. Yup, Lillith and family, stupid woman. Great, I am probably going to die here because this idiot trophy wife couldn't follow directions. If I die here, I hope I haunt her dumb butt. My wolf is pretty pissed off.

Looking down the hood the only plan I can come up with is to play bowling for zombies and try to not get bitten or run over. Not really counting on either. I slide down the hood into the front of the now angry and aggressive zombie pack using my toes more like a cats than a wolfs to launch myself into the middle. Landing heavily on top of several bodies, they fall easily under my weight. Scrambling to my feet, I muscle my way through the pack much the way I envision a sheep dog does a herd of cattle. Knocking them over as I move forward towards the check point entry as fast as I can. Avoiding teeth at this stage isn't too much of a problem as most of the moving dead are more focused on the larger noisier object but flailing limbs entangle me tearing bloody holes and they randomly grab pinch and pull.

Slipping in a puddle of.... whatever bodily fluid this is, I lose my footing and find myself underneath several of the recently felled zombies. The foul odor has completely clogged my nose and my ears aren't working well for some reason. My sight swims before me the only saving grace is their vehicle has stopped right on top of me. Panting and disorientated I feel a mouth close on my neck. With my nose not working I have no idea what's going on and in response my wolf spins onto its back forcing the intruder off of me. My eyes clear enough for my brain to recognize Bethy, fellow pack member, who has miraculously appeared.

The SUV speeds off, which distracts the vast majority of the still upright and mobile zombies. The dead to turn and take to a faster than normal shamble but not quite run after its hasty leave. However, that now leaves both Bethy and myself completely out in the open and exposed. I see my safe under car shady spot just feet away from us and give a quick yip while regaining my feet and dodging fallen zombie hands and teeth.

Understanding my meaning, she scrambles her way under it leaving room for me to scrape my belly but manage to crawl underneath as well. With hind limbs shaking and breath heaving I am on the verge of collapse. This heat is more than I can take any longer and though I am sure the neck wrap is useful, right now it just feels like a hot noose. I am bleeding from several open wounds some deep enough to concern me whether they are bites. I don't think I got bitten, but I wasn't really paying all that close attention to anything other than surviving. Bethy sniffs my many wounds but doesn't seem too concerned. I guess that's a good sign.

Now that the gates have re-closed, the excitement has died down and the zombies no longer have such a large and easy target they begin to lumber back towards the middle as if drawn in by some invisible queue. The problem was it seems to be in our general direction even with the occasional target practice the Arizona Guard seems to be throwing our way. With many more of the zombies knocked off their feet, they no longer have the brain power to get up but that doesn't stop these zombies are now crawling their slowly drying and burning flesh across the hot black rolled asphalt towards Bethy and I!

The return path to my escape hole is much too far for me. I am too unstable right now. Werewolves who get too hot or too hungry go into a kind of frenzy until they are restrained and the issue resolved, usually by friendly pack mates, or they just die. Bethy has neither the strength or size to restrain me, and then to what end. It's not like she's hiding an air conditioning unit or flank steak in her fur. I don't know what to do or where to go. I close my eyes in both a grimace of pain and panting from exhaustion and heat. Involuntarily my wolf snaps at Bethy attempting to drive her away from me. Her golden red coat now tar and goo covered, she simply stares at me with those piercing eyes. Ellan had for years treated her like one of the family, now here I was; threatening her life if not from my loosing control, to both of us getting mauled and mobbed by these already-dead dead.

A whistle sounds from behind us. Shifting on paws and belly's to see the cause, there is a small door open from a nearby restaurant. Now for anyone familiar with this Arizona California crossing this is still not a close thing. It is down the embankment towards the river, through a hedgerow and across a four foot chain link fence. Bethy bolts out covering half the distance before I can even get on my feet. She stops realizing I am not beside her. As a submissive wolf she shouldn't have taken the first lead, but I am too tired to care. She comes back, circling me, egging me on with little nips here and there. You'd think she was a cattle dog instead of a werewolf, but it is annoying enough to spur me to greater speed and haste.

We make is safely off the asphalt with the zombies reaction time being only enough for them to turn their bodies not change their actual movement. Part of me is thankful these aren't Amp'd up zombies or I'd be toast right now. Pushing our way through the hedgerow is simple enough, its rather sparse. But the fence, even at four feet is another matter for me. Gathering my hindquarters underneath me I make a first attempt and plant my face squarely into the top bar of the chain link. Falling, even from such a short distance, I land badly on my rump and hip letting out an involuntary yip. Werewolves are generally silent, so even I am surprised by the noise. I lay in the dirt looking at the still open door and Bethy just steps from it. I close my eyes. That's it I'm done. My heart beats an irregular rhythm, my hip hurts where I landed on it and my chest feels like an elephant sat on it. I close my eyes.

The hands that grab me, heave me over the fence and toss me unceremoniously as if I were no more than a bowling ball, sliding across a greased lane. I can hear Bethy grumble something but my world goes black.

Scott the Reluctant Hero

Waking up from my much needed rest, I can see that Josh the cop is almost gone. Almost one of the dead. I hear his heart faltering but still fighting and feel that the pounding of his blood no longer follows his veins but rather gathers into his lungs and belly. There must be some kind of tear somewhere, internal. I am no medic and there is nothing I can do to help him. But I got him home. In my entire life I have been discounted as a screw up, driven from my pack, taken from my home and made to live a solitary life. Neither as human nor wolf have I ever known comfort or peace. Maybe because he was dying or maybe because I was scared after the quake, but this man needed me. And more than that, somehow, he trusted me.

Watching him, he pulls out his little cop's notebook that somehow was still in his breast pocket. Opening its flip top cover, he begins to write on a blank page but all too soon, allows it to fall away from unfeeling hands. The pen and book may have slipped from his hands but he keeps mumbling. He says things like I love you. Tears start rolling from his eyes, sliding down his face to soak into the mattress. He no longer hears what he says even as the mumbling becomes softer and less distinct. This was a brave man, I think. A cop sure, but even in his pain and fear he treated me decently and spoke to me not like some dirty animal but as a person. I've rarely known that in my world.

He mentioned a sister in Arizona. She has a pack or is a werewolf or is somehow, I lose my train of thought as the last breath leaves him. Silent as the grave they say. I think I'll go and find this sister. I was always good at finding things. Taking and stealing things too. That's how this cop and his partner ran across me. I was trying to take the wallet out of one of the parked cars in the garage and they just happened to run a patrol through there. Not the first time I've been caught, but they treated me the nicest. No hitting me or knocking me to the ground. No stealing what I had rightfully stolen first. They took the wallet true, but only to run the ID through the identipad system, not to steal it for themselves.

Three days ago, had been just another day for me. Half-starving, broke and homeless, I had taken refuge in the long-term parking garage. Seemed safe enough. Wandering through, trying all the cars to see if any were open when I saw this wallet on the floorboard of a moderately priced four door sedan. Easy mark I thought. I pried open the door and to my surprise no alarm even sounded! I know I was grinning then. Sitting in the car after picking up the wallet, I was flipping through the contents when these two rolled up in their patrol car. Damn luck. They whooped their siren and lights at me, what was I supposed to do. They pulled me out, taking the wallet and ID after running the Vein Pattern Recognition only to come up blank. I had just been handcuffed, in the front I might add, when that earthquake hit. I had felt something, but it was so quick I didn't have time to react. Even the stray cats didn't have time to scatter. That's how I ended up on the ground three stories down. The one younger guy, I think Josh called him Dan, had died right away. Broken neck along with most of his ribs. I thought for sure Josh was dead. He looked dead. I myself, had what felt like a broken arm and dislocated shoulder in the fall. After you get enough beatings, you tend to know if the damage is critical or just painful; however changing not only allowed me to slip the cuffs but repair some of the damage since bones reshape and reform during the change. The shoulder just slipped neatly back into place while what is now one of my front legs, though super sore and tender, was no longer broken.

After effecting the change, I took off to find something to eat. I had used my nose to easily locate a broken and only partially buried vending machine. This day just kept getting better and better I remember thinking. Changing takes a lot of energy on the best of days and healing wounds only drains a werewolf further. I filled my belly full of chips, cakes and even a couple of real Slim Jims. Yum Yum. Werewolves become complete psychos if we get too hungry or too hot. I couldn't say why I went back to the dead officer and his partner. Maybe I was just lonely for company. Maybe I was still a bit scared.

My wandering mind returns to the now and I take a good look around the closed little single car garage. Although there are no working lights, some daylight still creeps through the metal door's edges giving my wolfs vision enough light to see by. A couple of mattresses, a washing machine and dryer on pedestals with a wash tub next to them, then a single door leading to the main house I presume. I put my nose down at the edge of this door breathing deeply. Yup, dead up there. Probably that family he was so keen to see again. The door handle is a lever rather than a knob, so my paws can easily open it. I figure since it swings in, I can slam it just as quick too, if need be.

Upon opening it, light floods the room from the outside to display a small set of old narrow cement stairs which I find lead to an equally narrow kitchen door that's standing open. That's never a good sign, I think. Slinking in, I make my way around the edge of a small but tidy kitchen with pristine cabinets. The farm house sink and pretty drapes over that sink show a fractured but not shattered window. In the corner is a water dispenser with its plastic five gallon half full bottle still on top. Making my way over there I allow myself to gorge on fresh clean water from the push button dispenser. Thankfully it's gravity fed, so no electricity needed.

Using my nose, I inhale deeply trying for any scent of the dead or werewolf. I never smelled wolf on either Josh or his partner, but I got the impression that his family might be somehow. Generally my encounters with other werewolves didn't end well, but a lone wolf is often a sad creature or a psychotic one. I'd been sad a very long time. The houses base scent was mostly cleaning products with a small amount of perfume. I could tell a total of four people had lived her Josh, a woman I presumed to be his wife and two not yet pubescent children. Teenagers have a musky dirty smell and these did not smell like that.

Padding my way around the rest of the small home, I count three tidy bedrooms, two minus their mattresses, yup checks out. The single oversized bathroom, equally as clean and so neat you could eat off those floors. Don't know who his wife was but I've never seen floors that clean. Following my nose, I enter Josh's bedroom and take a slow look around. Sweet pictures of the family adorn the walls along with a certificate from some college I've never heard of. I see a boy and a girl along with a woman I take to be his wife. Were they happy? Do people really get to be happy? Melancholy has been a long-time companion and one I really wished to shed.

Leaving the smiling faces, I pad back to the kitchen, satisfied that the dead I only weakly smell aren't actually in the home. Taking a moment to remember safety, I push closed the door leading back downstairs then make the mistake of opening the refrigerator with my nose. Ack, oh God! I back out trying my best not to wretch or make too much noise. Power must have been off this entire time; everything smells decayed and spoiled. I sneeze a few times to clear the odor from my snout. Once my sense of scent has returned, I feel reasonably safe to begin rummaging around in cabinets hoping for some food. They were a well-stocked family having crackers, chips, cereal and other easily accessible items. Score one for the hungry werewolf, I think.

Coming to a decision, I make my way back to Josh's bedroom pushing the door closed behind me. The change takes a really long time when you are injured and hurts more than usual. But I've been hurt before and this really isn't any more unusual for me oddly enough, than any other day.

Starting the change, you feel it at the base of the tail first. It is the oddest feeling for your tail; all this bone and sinew, to retract into the body. To go from flexible almost appendage to fused immovable bone. My hips shift to a seventy-degree angle before my legs fully reshape. The big bones of the thigh needing to change their attachments, knees needing to shift position as well. My muzzle reshapes while bones pop and break back into a round head shape rather than an elongated one. Several few drops of fluid leak onto their once pristine carpet. I vaguely feel embarrassed about this, though I couldn't say why. Muscles shrink and stuff themselves back into places hidden away. My hips shift once again this time not just in length but width, bringing with it pain and the usual shock. Fur transforms into hair and claws flatten to become nails. My vision is always the most startling to me. Seeing the colors as if for the first time back in human form. But in turn losing my sense of smell is a bit disconcerting.

Finally, my five-foot ten frame comes back into sharp focus bringing with it my one hundred and sixty pounds of flesh along for the ride. I'm by no means the largest wolf out there but neither am I small.

Still on my hands and knees, then standing carefully up on two feet for the first time in almost four days. The world spins for just a moment while I find my balance. Naked as a baby, I go rummaging through the closet for a shirt and pants. Experience has taught me his clothes will fit along with anything else I might need. Finding several pairs of tennis shoes I smile and slip a pair on. Holy smokes, there's a small amount of cash hidden in this pair of his sneakers. Instinctively I glance around as if the dead man could come and chastise me. Encouraged, my pace quickens as I check all of his pockets and other items to see if there is any more stashed away. Cash is always in short supply and I can only imagine out there with no electricity I'll need some.

In the middle of stuffing yet another small wad of bills into my newly pilfered jeans pockets I pause. In my brain an image flashes back to the dead man down below in the garage. A lump forms in my throat. I've never felt guilty about robbing anyone, let alone a dead cop. A flush comes unbidden to my cheeks. Returning to the kitchen I find a clean glass and again fill myself with the fresh water. Searching cabinets reveals a couple boxes of still good cereal. I gobble the first one down like a starving animal and in a way I am. I hadn't had any more food since the first day raid on the smashed vending machine. I tuck the opened second box under my arm and go to check out the computer desk drawer.

Like everything else in this home, the drawer is neat and tidy with an organizer in the front holding various pens, pencils, a utilitape and bingo – underneath is an old fashioned hand written spiral bound address book. Flipping through it is time consuming only because I find it macabre-ly interesting that beside each name, under each mobile number are notes. "Martha's mom" "Josh's best friend" "Handyman" I get down to the entry I was hoping I would find.

Liam & Ellan McCallen

623-555-0000

Josh's sister, kids Patrick and Jack

Underneath that are 4 neatly printed dates of birth along with an Arizona address, email and identi-mail.

I don't know when I decided to go find this family. This pack. Or why I would ever think they would do anything but rebuke me as my own family did. But I tear out the page and tuck it safely into the same pocket as all my freshly pilfered money from earlier. Finishing the second box of cereal I return to the bedroom to pack a travel bag of Josh-the-dead-cops-belongings-that-fit-me. Now to go steal a car. Is it really stealing if the owners dead? Guess we'll find out.

The Master Alpha Takes An Interest

The calls and texts come quick and furious. One after another. No less than a dozen to be sure. Everyone of them saying the same thing.

your son has been killed by the Phoenix pack

Gerry was a very, very old wolf. His only remaining son a few hundred years younger than him, but still by any account also a very old wolf. Falco was a born werewolf. Not a bitten in. As far as Gerry knew only a handful of werewolves could even claim that and the two American traveling packs were both led by natural borns.

Falco led the Festival Pack on the West Coast and Conan who was Falco's son and also a natural born led the Faire Haven pack on the East Coast. Each pack had agreements for safe travel between certain states and ran old time renaissance style fairs. And each pack stayed far away from the other as Conan had never gotten along with his father. But that was not surprising as Falco hadn't gotten along with his father either. And really to be honest, Falco hadn't gotten along with many people. He was a mean spirited greedy man who only saw value in the power he held as a werewolf Alpha. Ever covetous of his father, Falco desired both the title of Master Alpha as well as position. Gerry had long ago given up hope of redemption for his son. But he knew his grandson to be a reasonable and fair man that many liked.

Gerry was the long-time owner of the Southern California bar the Fiddle & Fang. Known for its good food, better atmosphere and great beer. It suited him. He no longer ruled a pack and had not done so for decades. But enough people came through the bar regularly that it fulfilled his wolfs need for family and pack. He honestly felt a bit surprised that so many wolves today even remembered there was such a thing as a Master Alpha. And more importantly, pretty sure he hadn't wanted the job for a good long time. Most days his amiable nature was at the forefront and that's how he liked it. The last time he lost his temper; the carnage had been noticeable even to the humans.

Having run the Fiddle and Fang pub for more years than even he remembered still gave him pleasure. It kept his nose to the ground always getting good and reliable information. First in Ireland, then as wars came and migration became necessary, here in America. Even with that, he'd had to pick up and move more than once. But change isn't what bothered the old wolf so much as loss and loosing those he knew and felt some measure of affection or guardianship over. These days his closest friend if indeed she could be called that was a rather diminutive solid black cat of some dubious morals. She wasn't as old he was, but had been a relatively constant companion over the last half millennium or so.

The old stained-glass windows both above the door and making both sides feel open yet secluded, are wavy and frosted with age; giving the pub a rather "charming" atmosphere according to local critics and tourists alike. But he knew the truth of how old they were and how hard it had been to preserve them all these years and through all the many moves. He probably could have bought a small island with the money it cost to transport them safely over the years.

The final straw came a few hours later after the texts had subsided, when a wolf came crawling in on all fours crying foul about how his son had been murdered in cold blood for no reason defending his pack mate. Now that he can't have. Listening to the submissive wolfs tale, he learns this all leads back to that upstart pup. The new Alpha of the phoenix pack Jack. He didn't know who he was, not really but he vaguely thought about the stories that had carried to him, remembering their alpha being a Mark something or other who had died just a year of so ago. Something about there being a spot of trouble in Phoenix last year with again stories coming back to him about cage fights, drugs being used on walking zombies and kidnapped wolves. Almost nobody shared gossip faster than a pack of wolves. Maybe he really should have gone down there and taken more of an interest. It being so close and all to his current location. A wolf on four paws could still manage the San Diego to Phoenix travel in a matter two to three days, driving could get him there in five hours. Maybe it's time he takes more of an active role. Yes, Gerry thinks putting his bar towel away and heading out the kitchens door.

Like all good bar keeps, he maintains his personal rooms above the bar. Taking the stairs a few at a time he puts plans in motion to attend to this wolf killing Alpha, named Jack. Pups need to be taught lessons. Some more severely than others.

TIME OF THE WOLF
ALICE E. WRIGHT

About the Author

Alice E Wright is a fan of the supernatural and her writing reflects her fondness for werewolves and vampires. Long-time resident of Arizona, she can often be found at science fiction/fandom/horror conventions and cat shows. She is a long time breeder of Siberian cats and author to several non-fiction cat informational books including The Raw Facts Of Feline Feeding, The Siberian Cat and coming soon What Your Pussy Cat Wants You To Know.

www.AliceEWrightBooks.com